Nicola Norton's debut novel, *On One Normal Night*, mixes ordinary lives with crime and mystery.

Nicola wrote this novel in her spare time whilst working and bringing up her two sons. She lives in Surrey and continues to ignite her passion for writing.

My family

N Norton

ON ONE NORMAL NIGHT

AUSTIN MACAULEY PUBLISHERS™

LONDON • CAMBRIDGE • NEW YORK • SHARJAH

A CIP catalogue record for this title is available from the British Library.

ISBN 9781787102163 (Paperback)
ISBN 9781787102330 (ePub e-book)

www.austinmacauley.com

First Published 2022
Austin Macauley Publishers Ltd®
1 Canada Square
Canary Wharf
London
E14 5AA

Prologue

Macy Reynolds was an ordinary girl with an ordinary life; until one day, that life was shattered by a cruel attack on her.

The lives of many people spiral out of control as number of suspects are interviewed and secrets and lies unravel. But who did attack Macy and will they ever be exposed?

Chapter 1

Yes! It was Friday at last. Get the work finished in the office and then off to the Admiral Arms! It had been a busy week at work and Macy was so looking forward to having her usual Friday night catch up with her friends, Lou and Ritchie.

They had been friends for some time now and Friday nights were their night to chill, relax and catch up with all the week's news at their local pub.

As Macy put on her coat to leave for work, she quickly checked herself in the mirror, "Yes Macy Reynolds, you look good to go!"

The sun was out as she headed for the train station; it looked like it was going to be a fine day.

Macy grabbed a coffee and waited for the train, she had done the same journey now for eight years but she enjoyed her job and never felt the need to work elsewhere.

HM Financial Services was based on the 11th floor of a modern skyscraper building in London. Macy's boss, Harry Matthews was a lovely man to work for. A big friendly person; kind, Grandad type of man, but stern when he needed to be.

Macy worked at her desk, dealt with phone calls, emails, clients, arranged meetings and managed the paperwork. It wasn't the best job in the world but it certainly wasn't the worst and having been there for some time, she felt like part of the furniture.

The train was busy today, Macy squeezed herself next to an elderly lady. *Only five stops and then a short walk to the office*, she thought.

Only two more hours to go and Lou would be finishing her shift at the hospital where she worked as a nurse.

Thursday was her night shift day so it meant she could go home Friday morning, sleep and then get up ready to catch up with Macy and Ritchie at the pub feeling refreshed.

Lou had known Macy since they had started at 'Welbeck High School'. Thrown together in a science class, sat at the back, they had formed a firm friendship of hating the lesson, sabotaging experiments and given that they were at the back of the class, being able to talk about celebrities, boys and fashion!

Both 28 now, their lives had taken on different paths but they still remained close and Friday night was Lou's favourite evening where she got to gossip with her best friend.

Doing what she loved most; caring for people, Lou had carved a career out of nursing and loved it. She didn't care about the long hours, night shifts or the low wage. She just wanted to make people feel better.

As the patients were just waking up, Lou was wheeling the medicine trolley into the ward. Mrs Simpson, a patient who had been in here for four days, lifted her head from her pillow. "Medicine time, my lovely," said Lou, "and then blood pressure. We are going to see if we can discharge you today, the doctor will be around shortly to assess you."

"Thank you, my angel nurse," said Mrs Simpson, leaning over for the cup of water. *Yes*, thought Lou, that's why she loved her job, for the appreciation from people like Mrs Simpson.

Ritchie Bart climbed into his delivery van – two deliveries down and eight more to go until knocking off time and a few drinks with the girls at the Admiral Arms.

Ritchie had been a member of this 'Friday Night Drinks Gang' since Lou had been his nurse and had cared for him, when three years earlier, he had suffered a traffic accident on a motorbike. She had nursed him back to good health and the two had become friends.

Through Lou, he had got to know Macy and the three had become rock solid, supporting each other through the good and bad times.

Setting off on his third delivery, Ritchie thought how he missed the openness and freedom of his motorbike. He had not ridden one since the accident and now had to make do with his van.

Nowadays, life was spent sat in traffic jams and dealing with a 30mph speed limit. Ritchie longed to be on a motorbike again, weaving in and out of traffic, getting to places much quicker than in his old blue van. Still, at least he had his health, friends and a job. He was grateful for that.

Chapter 2

The supermarket was busy today as Howard collected his basket from the front of the shop. Down the first aisle for bread and fruit, then onto the ready meals.

He surveyed the busy mums with their big trollies and the children in the seats at the front. Rushing down each aisle, trying to stop their children from grabbing food from the shelves into the trolley.

Sometimes it was a lonely life but after what had happened to him in 1993, he had resigned himself to the fact that he would never marry or have children.

Passing the herd of trollies that had been left at the end of the aisle where customers had left them to chat with each other, Howard strode down the alcohol aisle to put in his usual four cans of real ale.

Back outside, the sun had gone in now, and as he stepped back into the fresh air, he felt the breeze of the wind and buttoned up his coat. With his one carrier bag of shopping, Howard headed for the bus stop and home.

Guy Saunders stood outside the office lighting up his cigarette, a ten-minute break from looking at the computer screen. Still, at least it was Friday and he had Claire's birthday drinks at the pub tonight.

Claire worked alongside him in the office and was celebrating her 34th birthday today. Most of the office staff were going and he had been given 'a pass' from 'her indoors'! Innuendos aside, he admired his wife. She ran the house like clockwork, looked after their two children and generally held everything together while he worked long hours.

Putting everything into context, he probably had the easiest of lives and she didn't mind him having the odd night out. Inhaling the last of his cigarette, he put it out in the bin and walked through the revolving doors back into the office.

He stood for a while taking in the view from his window. He watched the traffic and the people milling about the roads and pavement. The bus stopped just opposite the office and Guy watched the crowd of people get off. An elderly gentleman caught his eye; it was the tweed of his coat that made him look familiar. His dad used to wear one very similar. He observed the old man – a single carrier bag in one hand and the other in his pocket, as he walked slowly towards the flats.

Macy looked at the clock, ten minutes until she could leave. She would answer the last four emails that she sat staring at on her computer, say goodbye to Harry and then head home. It wouldn't take her long to type the responses needed. After all the years in this job, she could now type quite quickly. Two more sentences and she would be done!

Macy re-tied her hair back up, grabbed her coat and headed for Harry's office. She said, "Bye Harry, have a lovely weekend with Beryl." Harry looked up from his desk, a wide smile appearing on his face.

"Bye, lovely, enjoy your drinks tonight. Beryl is cooking a curry tonight so I won't be leaving late tonight either."

12

"Aww lovely, Harry, see you Monday," and with that Macy breezed out of the door and headed for the train station.

Harry had grown so fond of Macy since she started working for him. She had flourished so much, becoming a confident, assertive member of the team. He remembered when she had first started; her now long brown hair had been short then and she had been timid and afraid of making any mistakes. He had shown her the ropes and given her his time and he had to admit she had been a fast learner and one of the best secretaries who had ever worked for him.

Shutting down his computer and locking the filing cabinet, he was glad it was Friday too.

Chapter 3

Macy quickly looked at her post before placing a pizza in the oven. A full stomach would stop her having a hangover tomorrow, she thought. With that in the oven, she jumped into the shower to wash away all of today's stress and get ready for tonight.

The gang usually met at about 7.30pm. That way, it gave Lou a chance to wake up and Ritchie and herself time to wind down from work.

Macy hadn't been a bit jealous to share Lou's friendship when she had been introduced to Ritchie. In fact, it had been refreshing to get to know him and have different conversations.

Lou had been good to him, giving up so much of her time to nurse him back to health. She remembered how Lou had been so proud of him when he had taken his first steps unaided, after so long in a hospital bed. Lou had been there for him too when he had returned home and helped him find a new routine. It had been a slow process for Ritchie but with determination and their good friendship with each other, he had managed to regain his independence and normality back again and he had slotted into the 'gang' very easily.

Stepping out of the shower, Macy flung a towel around her and headed for her bedroom to figure out her outfit for later. Macy had lived in her two-bedroom flat for nearly ten years now. It wasn't big or fancy but it was cosy and her neighbours were lovely.

She was on the ground floor with Mabel, a 76-year-old widow and there were four more flats above her on two more levels.

The building was nestled in between two huge willow trees and had a gravel path leading up to the main front door. The grounds were managed by a lovely man called Sid who came frequently to mow the grass, plant and generally maintain the greenery that enclosed the flats.

Eating a slice of pizza and applying mascara at the same time was trickier than Macy had thought. Sitting in front of her dressing table, plate perched on her lap, Macy carefully brushed her lashes with the wand.

She finished the pizza and walked to her bed, surveying the clothes she had decided on earlier. The skirt and jumper would do, as she glanced at her clock.

She had a bus to catch! Pulling on her tights, then her skirt and cream jumper with frills on the sleeves, Macy applied her pink lipstick and brushed her hair. There, she was ready. Zipping up her boots and locking the door behind her, she headed to the bus stop.

Lou turned the corner into Admiral Avenue and walked along the pavement, passing the many, now closed, shops. She lived nearest the pub and always met the others outside; on the benches they provided for when the weather was hot enough to sit outside. She was looking forward to tonight as she had some exciting news to tell her friends.

Nearing the benches, Lou noticed she would be the first to arrive as they were all unoccupied. She didn't mind waiting as she could see the bus stop and would be able to see Macy as the bus pulled in.

Lou glanced at her watch, the bus should arrive in about seven minutes, so familiar they were with this routine on a Friday, that Lou knew the bus times off by heart. She sat and waited.

Ritchie jumped into his van and started the engine; it would only take him ten minutes to get there. He was on so many tablets that he only ever had one beer, then stuck to soft drinks and the pub had a carpark so it was easier for him to just drive.

He turned into the Avenue just as the bus was stopping on the other side of the road. He watched Macy get off and walk the few steps to meet Lou by the benches. With his indicator flashing, he drove into the carpark.

Chapter 4

The Admiral Arms was one of those old-fashioned pubs, patterned carpet, dark red walls and embellished wallpaper.

Bar stools lined the L shaped bar and unmatching tables and chairs covered the carpet area. There was a small wooden floor area where resident bands stood and played ballads on a Saturday night. It was popular with locals, but also new clientele frequented there sampling the vast amount of wines on offer and different real ales on the pumps.

The three of them, after saying their 'hellos' outside walked in; it was busy tonight. Ritchie always bought the first drink while the girls found somewhere to sit.

They found a table just to the left of the bar with a good view of the rest of the pub and the entrance.

"How's your week been, Macy?" asked Lou, as the girls removed their coats and got comfortable. "Yeah good, thanks, same old same old at work, but good."

Ritchie at this point joined them balancing a pint of beer, a bottle of wine and two glasses. He pulled the chair out between the two girls and sat down. "So, what's the gossip this week then?" he asked.

Ritchie had three older sisters, so had grown up in a very dominant female household and was very confident and comfortable around women.

"Well, I have some exciting news," said Lou, as she poured the wine into both glasses.

"Oooooo," squealed Macy, "tell us more."

Lou went on to tell the pair that she had been offered a promotion at work, to become a sister in the ward where she worked. If she went for it, of course she would be a fool not to, she would have an interview in two weeks.

Ching ching, went the three glasses as all three friends raised their glasses in excitement and anticipation of the happy news Lou had just shared. "That's fantastic!" said Macy, her face glowing. "I'm so pleased for you and of course you will smash the interview!"

As the three caught up with other news, the background music became louder and the pub busier.

To the right of the bar and round the corner, Claire's birthday drinks were going well. Most of the office had turned up and Guy was on his third drink already. He had gone to the pub straight from work, so was still in his suit but had removed his tie and unbuttoned his shirt.

He was standing in a group with his boss and two others. His boss was trying his best to be funny telling jokes and Guy found his mind and eyes wandering. He had never been to this pub before; he and his wife were more restaurant goers now, preferring a meal out when they had the luxury of finding a babysitter.

His days of going out drinking and becoming drunk were long gone; especially when there was no chance of laying in the morning.

The pub was busy, and Guy's eyes flitted from one group of people to the next. He watched a group of young lads larking about near the entrance. Obviously, some kind of football team as they all wore the same sports jackets on which bore the emblem 'Radcliffe Rovers'.

There were couples at tables for two, bigger groups of friends that just stood, glasses in hand and men and women like him, he guessed, that had just come straight from work in office-type clothes.

He stared at the other end of the bar, two girls and a man were chatting vigorously and laughing. The girl with the long brown hair caught his eye and he realised he must have been staring for quite a while. He turned away from her gaze quickly and surveyed the people on the bar stools. His gaze stopped at a lone man perched by the bar. He looked familiar but Guy could not place where he had seen him before.

His daydreaming came abruptly to an end when he realised his two female colleagues were in fits of laughter at his boss and he was asked why he wasn't laughing.

Howard didn't always come to the pub on a Friday, if ever really. He sometimes came in on weekdays for a bite to eat and a drink. Tonight though, he felt he didn't want to sit in on his own watching the same old television programmes; he felt the urge to do something different.

Sipping his drink, Howard nodded to the lad next to him who was ordering a lot of drinks. "Are you the unlucky one, getting lumbered with paying for all those?"

"Nah mate, we have a kitty, I'm just the unlucky one tonight that's in charge of the money," answered the young man. He lifted the tray from the bar and Howard watched as he walked to the table near the door and handed out the drinks.

Must be some sort of club or something, thought Howard, thinking how nice it must be to belong and have a sense of belonging.

Billy Tomlin stuffed the change from the round into his pocket. He would have to get more money from everyone soon if they carried on drinking as fast as they were.

Radcliffe Rovers football team trained every Friday evening at the park adjacent to the pub for two hours before crossing the street and finishing their night in the Admiral Arms.

Billy, a 24-year-old scaffolder, had been with the team now for 18 months and enjoyed the social side of it. Wednesday's and Friday's training and then a match on Sunday. It filled up most of his spare time but he didn't care; he loved football and had made new friends since joining the team and the team were celebrating tonight after a 4–0 win last Sunday, which had put them top of the league!

"Oooo, has someone an admirer at the bar?" said Lou nudging Macy. "He has been staring at you for a while."

"No!" said Macy, feeling slightly uncomfortable. She had felt the stranger's gaze and for whatever reason it had made her feel uneasy.

Macy quickly changed the subject and turned her chair inwards slightly. "What's everyone's plans for the weekend then?"

"Nothing," replied Ritchie, "Netflix and junk food!"

"I'm working Sunday," chipped in Lou, "so some retail therapy for me tomorrow." she grinned.

The bell rang and Mike the landlord shouted, "Last orders, folks!" It was at this time that the pub began to empty out somewhat, either people going home or going on somewhere else to continue their night out.

"Right, who wants a lift?" asked Ritchie. Lou put her thumbs up as she drank the last of her drink.

"No worries, Ritchie, I'll get the bus. I still have 15 minutes until the last bus arrives, and anyhow I'm going in the opposite direction."

"You sure Macy, it's no problem," said Ritchie pulling on his coat.

"It's fine thanks, the fresh air will sober me up a bit," laughed Macy.

Only on the odd occasion did she get a lift home from Ritchie. She lived in the opposite direction for one thing, and the other was that she thought it a liberty to rely on him for lifts just because he didn't drink as much alcohol as her and Lou. She was fine getting the bus anyhow.

Struggling to squeeze past the now very loud football team, Macy, Lou and Ritchie said their goodbyes and Macy headed for the bus stop.

Guy had had enough too, others from the office were heading to the 'late' 'late' bar, but after a day's work and an evening drinking, he was whacked. Having not driven to work today because of this tonight, he would have to catch the bus home. Picking up his briefcase, Guy headed for the door.

Howard contemplated another drink but on the reasoning that he would have to rush it, he had left the pub and was at the bus stop waiting to catch the last bus home. From the bus stop, he could see all the customers leaving the pub, most much louder and more unsteady than when they entered.

Groups of girls were giggling and falling about, the large group of men in matching jackets were also leaving, a handful of them stopping to chat up the girls.

The sound of heels clip clopping made Howard turn his head away from the pub to see a young girl with *long brown* hair approach the bus stop and sit on the seat provided next to him. He shuffled up slightly and crossed his legs.

"See you Sunday, mates," swayed Billy.

"10 o'clock sharp for kick off," shouted Robbie, captain of the team.

Billy thought about walking home but after consuming so much alcohol, he thought the bus was the easiest option. He crossed the road to the bus stop.

Guy stood behind the bus shelter and reached in his pocket for his phone. Although his wife would be asleep, he felt it was best to text her saying he was getting the bus and would be home within 30 minutes. Just as he pressed send, he could see the headlights of the bus arriving down the street.

Chapter 5

Macy sat near the exit door on the bus on a seat for two. She placed her bag down on the spare seat next to her in the hope that she wouldn't have to move it for someone to sit there. She was tired now and ready for bed. She rested her head on her hand; not long now and she would be tucked up in bed fast asleep.

Billy staggered onto the bus and stood holding the rail. He could have sat if he wanted to as the bus was not busy, but he preferred to stand fearing that if he sat, he would fall asleep and miss his stop.

A man brushed past him with a briefcase. "Sorry," he said.

"No worries, mate," slurred Billy.

Macy glanced up and noticed it was the man that had been staring at her in the pub. She turned away quickly to look out of the window and noticed in the reflection of the glass that he had sat behind her.

Somehow, the gentleman that had been first at the bus stop came onto the bus last. He had ushered Macy to go on before him and she figured that the other two guys must have pushed in front of him too.

Showing his bus pass to the driver, Howard worked his way to the back of the bus. No one was sitting across the back seat which suited Howard. He preferred not to have to make small talk with anyone at this time of night.

Guy realised the lady in front of him had been the girl who had caught his eye in the pub earlier, just as the bus drove away from the kerb. He recognised her long hair and could see the side of her face in the window. He wished now that he had sat a bit further away from her; he didn't want her to think that he was some sort of crazy fella! It would look even more odd too, if he moved seats now.

At the next stop, two young girls got on, giggling and chatting. Macy could still hear them as they sat down to the right of her. She grinned to herself as she thought about all the times Lou and her had giggled like that and still did.

For the next two stops, no one entered the bus nor got off from it. The girls had stopped laughing now and the only noise you could really hear was the engine of the bus.

Macy's phone beeped and she opened her bag to reach for it. It was Lou, saying she was home and thank you for a lovely night as always. Macy replied with a thumbs up emoji and a kiss. Two more stops and a short walk and she would be home too.

As Macy got off the bus, so too did one or two others. For some reason she felt slightly vulnerable and quickened her pace, not attempting to look behind her although she could hear footsteps.

Rationally thinking now, she knew she was being silly as she walked up her pathway but she tightened the grip on her handbag nevertheless. Anyway, no one was going to be behind her now; this was where she lived and she could no longer hear footsteps.

Passing the big willow trees, Macy gasped as a gloved hand came in front of her covering her mouth and another hand punched her hard at the back of her head. Her legs buckled beneath her and then it all went dark.

Chapter 6

Macy woke to a blurring of blue and white sky and an incredible pain to the back of her head. For a while she thought she had woken up to an horrific hangover, but then it all came back to her.

No, no, this couldn't be happening, she thought, trying to get up. The pain in her head was overbearing and she felt disorientated. Where was she? Slowly she sat up and realised she was under one of the willow trees and turning her head she could see the window of her flat.

She could hear the birds singing and a noise of faint traffic in the background. It must be the early hours of the morning.

Macy touched the back of her head and winced, she had a lump the size of an egg there but seemingly, no blood. Had she fallen? Had she been so drunk that she couldn't walk? No, she hadn't drunk that much and she always made it home, no matter what.

Thinking made her hurt more and the best thing she needed to concentrate on was getting inside her flat; even if it meant crawling on her hands and knees, she had to get indoors.

Only then did she look down and notice her skirt. tights and knickers round her ankles.

Macy gagged and struggled not to be sick. It was now that the realisation set in. Unable to control herself, she started sobbing and knew the pain she had was not just hurting from her head.

Big sobs just kept coming until Macy had nothing left to give. What was she meant to do now and who had done this to her?

Macy slowly rose to her feet, pulling her knickers up, her tights were torn and the top of her thighs bruised.

A small light glistened from the grass ahead of her and Macy could see it was the buckle from her clutch bag. Taking a few small steps, she picked it up. Her purse, lipstick and keys were there, but what if he had been in her flat? Used her keys and then put them back?

Macy knew she had to go indoors, but she was frightened. She was frightened of being out here too. Putting one foot in front of the other, she slowly made her way home.

Twisting the key in the lock, Macy opened the front door. Strangely, all that hit her was the smell of the pizza that she had cooked the night before.

Placing her bag on the table in the hallway, she slowly made her way to the living room. All was how she had left it; it seemed whoever had done this to her, had not entered her flat.

Gagging again, probably partly this time with relief and also with the pain, Macy stumbled to the kitchen and retched into the sink. She scooped back her hair and stood motionless for what seemed like hours, but in reality, it was probably only a few minutes.

What happened now? Macy looked down at herself; she needed a shower. She felt grubby, dirty, ashamed. Would anyone believe her or would they just think she was a dirty, cheap, drunken slag? The tears came again. She wanted to scream!

Lou! She would phone Lou, she would know what to do being her best friend and a nurse, she would know exactly what to do.

Macy cleared her throat, drank some water straight from the tap and slowly walked to get her bag from which she pulled out her phone.

Macy noticed her hands were shaking and muddy as she found Lou's number. "Hello you, how you feeling today?" Lou's cheerful voice echoed in Macy's head. She tried to speak but the words wouldn't come. How do you tell your best friend that you think you have been attacked and raped?

"Hello, hello, Macy, it is you there isn't it?" Lou's voice becoming less cheerful and more concerned. In a small fragile whisper Macy muscled up the courage and replied,

"Lou, help me please, I need you to come over…now, its urgent. I'm hurting…"

The tears came uncontrollably now.

"I'm coming," said Lou. Macy put the phone down and waited. She didn't sit or move until the intercom buzzed, to which Macy ran, opened the door and literally fell into Lou's arms.

Lou sat and held Macy as she relived her ordeal and tried to make sense of what was unfolding. Tears trickled down her face as Macy showed her the bruises on her thighs and the lump to her head.

Why hadn't she made her get into the van with Ritchie? Why had she been so stubborn as to refuse the lift and catch the bus instead? How much had they drank?

She looked at her friend – still dressed in last night's clothes; bedraggled, lost and hurt; she had wanted to sob, but she had to be strong now, let the feelings come later. Macy had called her first and she had to help. *Put your professional head on, Lou*, she thought.

"We need to bag up your clothes, Macy, but don't shower, just put on clean ones as the police will need to examine you for evidence. It will be awful, Macy, but we need to do this to catch the evil person who did this to you. I'll be right with you all of the time."

Macy nodded, grateful for her friend to take over; it allowed her not to have to think, which eased her pain so very slightly.

She removed her clothes and caught sight of herself in the mirror. She noticed small bruises around her wrists as well, which meant he had held her down. Feeling sick again Macy tried to concentrate on getting dressed. Although still having not had a shower, Macy felt cleaner in fresh jogging bottoms and a sports top. She winced as she bent over to tie up her trainers. "Nearly ready," she whispered.

They arrived at the police station fairly quickly. Macy had never been in one before, only having seen them on TV. It was different in real life – lighter, cleaner maybe.

Lou led her to the desk. "Good morning," said Lou to the tall, uniformed man that stood before them. "last night my friend was attacked and raped, we need to talk with someone please."

Lou thought she sounded assertive and in control, but inside her heart was breaking for her friend. Macy looked so vulnerable standing there.

The man wrote something down and looked at Macy. In a quiet voice he said, "Take a seat, ladies, someone will be down straight away for you."

Chapter 7

"Macy Reynolds?" A tall, blonde woman, probably in her early forties stood opposite Macy and Lou. She was wearing navy trousers with small kitten heels and a white and blue striped shirt. Macy thought she had kind eyes.

"Yes that's me," replied Macy.

"I'm Detective Inspector Leanne Atkins," said the woman placing herself down next to Macy. Speaking quietly, she explained that Macy had done the correct thing by coming here as soon as she could. She told Macy that they were going to a room where she would ask questions, then some nurses would take her along the corridor to be examined. That she would take the bag of clothes for the forensics to look at too. Her voice was quiet, but reassuring and Macy felt at ease with her.

"Can my friend be with me?" shivered Macy, realising the full impact of what was about to happen.

"Of course," answered Leanne, "and if at any time you need a break, just say."

She led Macy and Lou into a room which had one sofa and two chairs. Leanne beckoned the girls to the sofa. There was a small table and a drinking water machine. The walls were mint green and there was a painting on the wall of a countryside scene. Macy wished upon anything that she was there in that picture, in the cottage amongst the trees, with the red tall poppies that grew between the lush green grass. To be anywhere but here.

A knock at the door drew Macy away from her daydream. In walked a man of medium stature, probably younger than DI Atkins, with dark, short hair.

"This is my colleague, DS Dan Evans," said DI Atkins. "He will be sitting in on this interview and writing down everything you tell us. Is that OK?" Macy nodded her head as DS Evans sat in the remaining chair next to DI Atkins.

Amongst tears, tissues and Lou's support, Macy answered their questions as best as she could, trying to remember every single detail about the night. She told them about the pub, what she could remember of who was in there, about Lou and Ritchie, about waiting for the bus, being on the bus, getting off the bus and walking to her home which she never reached.

All the time, DI Atkins was patient, understanding and sympathetic, never making her feel like she was the one who was to blame. DS Evans nodded and wrote down every fact.

"Tell us about when you woke up, where you were, how did you feel, tell us exactly what you did. Please Macy, step by step," said DI Atkins. Macy went through everything, her head hurting, her ripped tights, her bag on the grass, staggering indoors and ringing Lou. It was awful saying it out loud realising that she had been attacked, raped and left all night, just to satisfy someone's sick pleasure, but she knew she had to be strong and let the police know everything.

After, she was taken to another room, one now that looked like a doctor's surgery. Clinical and clean with a bed, sink and a first aid cabinet in.

Macy was told to strip down to her underwear first, where two nurses took pictures of her bruises and her head. She then had to have swabs taken from underneath her fingernails and in her mouth. The nurses were gentle and kind, telling Macy exactly what was happening at all times.

Then came the bit which Macy had been dreading but knew had to happen. She slowly took her knickers off and lay down on the bed. Lou was just at the other side of the curtain; it would all be over with soon. The nurses chatted but it was all a bit of a blur to Macy. She gritted her teeth and let them do what they had to.

They gave Macy some cream to ease the pain and said the bump to her head would subside in a few days. She was given leaflets about helplines for this sort of thing and was taken back to DI Atkins and DS Evans.

"Well done, Macy, you have been brilliant. Go home, have a shower and rest. We will start our investigation straight away and be in touch with you. Any worries or concerns, please ring this number." DI Atkins handed over a card to Macy. "It's my mobile number and work number for here; don't hesitate to ring me, but we will keep you updated with everything we are doing."

"Thank you," mumbled Macy. She and Lou were led to the exit and Macy had never been so grateful to get out into the fresh air as she was now. She turned to Lou and burst into tears; a mixture of relief, sickness and fear overwhelming inside of her.

Chapter 8

The shower felt warm and comforting against her body. Macy scrubbed and scrubbed wanting every inch of her body cleansed from whoever had done this to her. The water ran over her fast and powerful and she didn't want it to end. Her headache had almost gone and she didn't feel so shaken anymore but the sickness in the pit of her stomach just would not leave her.

Would there be any clues to help the police? Would whoever had done this, feel guilty and hand himself in? Had he done this before or had she been his first? Would he do it again? Was it someone she knew? All these questions and at the moment no answers; just physical pain and mental stress.

Macy had to let the police get on with their job and she had to concentrate on getting better. She turned off the shower and grabbed a towel. Lou would be waiting for her in the living room.

Lou had busied herself whilst Macy had been showering. She had moved magazines and papers about—not really tidying but keeping occupied. She had made tea and a sandwich for them both, not that she really felt hungry as she was sure Macy wouldn't be either, but what else was she to do? She felt helpless for her friend.

Macy came into the lounge wearing leggings and a T shirt. Lou felt she looked vulnerable and with her hair tied up and make-up free, much younger than her 28 years.

"Sandwich and tea," said Lou. Macy drunk the tea but picked at the sandwich, not feeling the urge to want to eat anything. It felt that every tiny mouthful got stuck at the back of her throat. Lou sensing this, got up. "What about soup, Macy? Have you any I can make for you?"

"I don't feel like having anything to be honest, Lou," replied Macy.

"Another cuppa then?" Lou went to put the kettle on.

"Come and stay with me, Macy," Lou offered. "I can take the week off work and you should ring Harry to let him know you won't be in."

Macy stared in disbelief; Harry, work, yes the world was still up and running and she didn't feel part of it anymore, and the worse part was she was going to have to tell people what had happened to her. How? What? When? Her parents?

As soon as Macy and her brother had moved out and had forged their own lives, Macy's Mum and Dad had moved to Spain, enjoying their retirement in the sunshine. Macy spoke to them about once a month and had visited and holidayed there about three times in the six years they had been there.

No, she wouldn't worry her parents with this right now, and her brother lived in Ireland with his young family, so there was nothing he could do. However, she would have to tell Harry, as she was expected in at work on Monday and she guessed she would have to tell Ritchie too.

Just as the kettle boiled, the intercom on Macy's flat buzzed making her jump back to reality. It was DI Atkins, DS Evans and a team of people in white overalls.

"Hi, Macy," said DI Atkins, "sorry to have to do this so soon but we need to survey the area where you were attacked as there may be DNA and fresh evidence. Can you come and show me exactly where you walked and where you woke up this morning, please?"

Macy pulled on her trainers and retraced her steps from the night before. The whole area had been cordoned off and Macy could see her neighbours looking out and curtains twitching. She felt embarrassed and emotional. Sensing this, DI Atkins quietly said, "Macy, we will have to question your neighbours to inquire whether they saw or heard anything, OK?" Macy nodded, she guessed no one had; she was certain that someone would have alerted the police or helped her if they had.

"Guv," shouted a man in a white overall. "OK, Macy, you go back inside now," said DI Atkins and she made her way to the spot where the man was pointing to.

Macy walked back inside; what had they found? It was clear she wasn't to know yet. She tried so hard to remember anything about her attacker, but she had nothing. All she could remember was a hand around her mouth and then darkness. If only she had turned her head to look behind her, would she have seen him then? Had he covered his face? She just didn't know but needed to. She hoped the police would catch him as she needed to know who had done this to her.

DI Atkins looked down at the spot to where the guy was pointing to. She bent to have a closer look at what was shining up at her; small, but there glistening in-between the blades of grass; a white shiny button stared back at her.

"Bag it up, well done," said DI Atkins.

"Looks like a shirt button, guv, probably from the cuff," said the guy.

Yes, thought DI Atkins, *possibility number one: were they looking for a professional person, office type kind of man?* she wondered.

Chapter 9

Billy woke that morning, or rather midday, with a thumping headache. God, they had all drunk somewhat last night but it had been a great evening. *The lads were a good crack,* he thought as he poured himself a glass of water and reached for the paracetamol.

Not that he had much to do today, he could go back to bed, but he didn't want a banging hangover to spoil the rest of his weekend. *Paracetamol and a bacon sarnie would do the trick*, he thought.

As he reached in the fridge for the bacon, he noticed some scratches on his hand. *That's odd*, he thought, must have done them at work and he had only just noticed. Gulping down the water and waiting for the bacon to grill, Billy put his clothes from last night into the washing machine and sat down.

Guy was down the park with his children and wife, earlier than he had wanted to be. He would have liked to have laid in this morning but no chance when you had kids; those lazy Saturday mornings were long gone. He wasn't used to these late nights and drinking sessions straight from work.

Sensing that he was tired, Lucy, Guy's wife, took over from pushing the buggy and beckoned her husband to the nearby bench opposite the lake. Their older child was scooting around them.

"You must be feeling it today," she grinned, "getting home in the early hours of the morning!"

Guy turned to her, "You heard me come in, then? I thought you were asleep?"

"I stirred when I heard the key in the lock and had a sneaky peek at the clock," replied Lucy. "Mind you, it was a long while after you sent the text saying you were on the bus," she winked, "Did you sneak back to the pub?" Lucy laughed and Guy mumbled something back, though she wasn't quite sure what as the noise from the scooter, the ducks on the lake and the breeze made it difficult for her to hear him.

Back at the station, the 'button' was being examined and DI Atkins was briefing the rest of the team whilst DS Evans was attaching a photo of Macy to the whiteboard.

"First things first, we have observed and searched the area where Macy was attacked. The only thing found was a white pearlescent button which is being looked at as I speak. Apart from that there are no obvious clues. We need to interview the neighbours where Macy lives, speak to the landlord of the Admiral Arms, the pub Macy was in yesterday evening and interview as many people as we can who were drinking in there at that time." DI Atkins flung the folder down and reached for her coat. "Fancy a swift half?" she laughed as she and DS Evans headed for the pub.

Howard had had an easy morning. He had pottered down to the newsagents to get the paper and some bread for his lunch and was now sitting down to do the crossword. He usually started it on a Saturday and dipped in and out of it when he felt like it to continue and complete it. This was as exciting as his weekends had become nowadays. Crossword, TV and a trip to the local shops. Still, he was happy enough in his own little world; not really needing or interfering with anyone. Howard the loner, that's what he was sure everyone around here called him. He didn't mind that though, it was better than the other name he was labelled with a few years ago and before he had moved here to get away from it all.

Chapter 10

The Admiral Arms was quiet for a Saturday afternoon; in the corner a few locals sat around a TV screen which was showing a football match and a few small groups of people occupied the tables.

DI Atkins and DS Evans headed towards the bar. Showing the gentleman behind the bar their ID cards, they explained what they were doing there.

Mike, taken aback by what he had just heard, ushered the detectives out to the back room which was made up of a dining table and chairs and a small sofa opposite a little TV on a stand.

They all sat, "Tea? Cof*fee?*" offered Mike.

"No, thanks," they both replied in unison.

"It was busy last night," spoke Mike. "heaving in fact, we had the usual locals in, 'Friday night out' people, an office party and a football team of some sort. It was loud and manic but nothing odd about it."

DI Atkins showed Mike a photo of Macy. "Yes, I recognise her, comes in with another girl and a bloke most Fridays. Seems like a nice girl, how awful." Mike's head lowered as he thought about her and what had happened when she had left his pub. *Terrible people in the world we live in*, he thought.

As he relived the evening, he gave the detectives every bit of information they asked for and said that he would be in touch if he thought of anything more that they would be interested in.

DI Atkins and DS Evans left the pub and returned to the car. "Right, we have lots of people to get hold of and I think we need to speak to Macy's other friend who was with her. Lots to do, no rest for the wicked," said DI Atkins as she turned on the engine.

"No weekend for us then!" replied DS Evans.

Macy didn't sleep a wink that night at Lou's; last night's events churning around in her head and stomach. She had put off phoning Harry, telling Lou she would do it tomorrow. She clenched her fists and closed her eyes tight, as if that would help her remember something more. No, nothing, she relaxed her body and turned over. *"Ow,"* she said out loud, remembering she couldn't sleep that way because the bump on her head hurt too much when she put any pressure on it.

Hold on, Macy sat bolt upright in bed. It was as if a flash had turned on inside her brain. That man, in the pub who had been staring at her, he had been on the bus too. What if he had followed her and attacked her? She felt sick. He hadn't looked like a sex attacker but what were they meant to look like anyway?

She reached for her bag and pulled out the card that DI Atkins had given to her when she had left the police station. Macy looked at her phone; it was just after half past 12. Was it too late to phone her? She had said anytime but this was taking the mick. DI Atkins could be out even, or relaxing indoors or worse still, have children in bed and Macy would wake them by ringing her now.

No, she had to ring her. She had to say this out loud and share this memory that had made her sit bolt upright. Who was he and why had he been staring at her? Had he been thinking exactly what he was going to do and followed her to the bus stop knowing exactly how her night was going to end? She dialled the number.

Chapter 11

DI Atkins turned over in bed and reached for her phone, her eyes not yet fully opened and her brain not yet fully engaged to see the screen to be aware of who was calling her so late in the night.

"Hello," she tried to sound fully awake and alert but in all honesty, she was shattered after working all day today. In fact she had only arrived home just before 10.30pm, after completing paperwork.

"Sorry to call so late," hesitated Macy, "but I have remembered something about somebody in the pub and on the bus. It may be nothing but I feel it's important that I tell you."

"No problem," said DI Atkins feeling more with it now and sat up in bed. Macy explained about the man in the Admiral Arms who seemed like he could have come straight from work as he was in a suit and how he had sat behind her on the bus. DI Atkins listened intrigued by this information. The shirt button playing on her mind. "Do you know where he got off the bus?" she asked Macy. Macy was stumped. He hadn't got off before her, had he? No, she was sure, but had he left the bus at her stop or had he stayed on it? She was confused now.

"A couple of people got off behind me at my stop but I'm afraid I can't remember if it was him." She felt stupid now, ringing DI Atkins up at this time and then not being able to answer her questions accurately enough. The tears fell again.

"Don't worry, Macy, this information you have remembered is important and we will find this man and interview him. Just telling me that he was in the pub and on your bus is vital to us, and what he was wearing as well," reassured DI Atkins.

She put the phone down; she had to find this man. At the moment he was the lead suspect – the button, him in a suit, on the bus at the same time as Macy. Could he have followed her? It all added up but it could also mean finding him and the button not being a match which would eliminate him. Who knew? What she did know was that he needed to be found and quickly.

Macy tossed and turned the rest of the night. Her head beginning to hurt again where the painkillers were probably wearing off and the fact that every time she closed her eyes, she saw herself waking up under that willow tree half naked, scared and alone. This was no dream; it was a nightmare that was real.

Chapter 12

The sunlight crept in through the curtains as Harry and Beryl awoke. Sundays were 'easy' days for them both. Later, after a cooked breakfast, they had a nice brisk walk through the woods opposite their newly built detached house.

Harry had worked hard for this and Beryl and himself had always yearned to own a house in the country somewhere, so when he had found out about these six new buildings being built three years ago just out of town and heading towards countryside, he had bought one. With his own children having flown the nest, he and Beryl didn't really warrant the five-bedroom house in town anymore. It was too big for just the two of them, so this three-bedroom house was perfect.

Enough room for themselves, with two small bedrooms spare for when the children and grandchildren came to stay.

Harry pulled the curtains back and looked across at the fields and trees. *Bliss*, he thought. OK, so it was further for him to travel to work but a view like this made getting up half an hour earlier in the week worthwhile.

The buzzing of his phone made him awake from his daydream. *Macy*, he thought, *how strange, she never rings at the weekends.* Harry listened intently and Beryl realised it must be important as he had turned his back to her and his voice was quiet and serious.

"Take as long as you need, Macy, and really if there is anything I can do…" grimaced Harry. He placed the phone down on the dressing table and stood still for a second, just to digest everything Macy had just told him. No longer taking in the magnificent view but still facing the window, he felt numb and sickened. How could someone have done this to Macy? She was the nicest, kindest person in his office and she always bought him the particular toffees he liked as a treat.

"You look like you have seen a ghost!" commented Beryl, as he slowly turned his body away from the window. Explaining everything to Beryl, Harry sat with a cup of tea, holding the warm mug in his hands. Feeling the warmth gave him some sort of comfort from this mad horrible world he resided in.

DI Atkins and DS Evans had to manoeuvre round the buses in the depot before they came to a cabin which they guessed was 'the office'. DS Evans tapped on the door.

"Come in," said a gruff voice from inside.

As they entered, the man sat upright from the slumped position he had been in; these people looked important. Explaining why they were there, the man went to a filing cabinet and pulled out lots of papers. "Friday night you say."

"Yes," replied DI Atkins, "bus 510 and the route which stops yards from the Admiral Arms. Between 11.30pm to midnight."

The man shuffled with the papers. "Ah, here it is, Terry Walker is the driver you want. He was driving the bus that night. Though he isn't due back in until tomorrow, he has the weekend off."

"OK, an address for him please." This time the man headed towards another filing cabinet. With address in hand, it was time to find Terry Walker.

Chapter 13

Terry had been a bus driver for 13 years; it was convenient for him. No stress, not much paperwork and working shifts meant he was around some days to take and collect his children from school which he loved.

He had three children, two boys and a girl, and being a dad was what he relished most. Although, at 15, 14 and 11, his days of being needed were almost through. It was only the 11-year-old now that needed taking and picking up from school; the other two, ironically, caught the bus.

Terry enjoyed the night shifts as well when the roads were quieter and the bus less busy. He was glad to have the weekend off after a busy week at work. He had the house to himself too as the wife was at lunch with her sister, his older children with friends and his youngest at football training. He was just about to go into the garden to do some weeding when he heard the front door knocker.

He was astounded to see two police officers on the doorstep and his first thought was for his children's safety or stupidity! After being reassured that everyone in his family were safe, DI Atkins explained why they were there.

Terry led them into the kitchen where they all sat around a solid wooden table. Declining a hot drink which Terry had offered them, he sat down.

Having had time to think back to Friday night, he remembered clearly the bus stop they were talking about near the Admiral Arms Pub. He had been in there a couple of times himself. Terry relayed what he could remember. "I can recall the bus stop," he said, "especially as an older gentleman let a girl get on before him, then the younger lads, probably from the pub, pushed past him too. You see it all the time in my job. People who have no patience to queue."

Bringing him back to the information they really needed, DI Atkins showed him a photo of Macy. "Was this the girl?"

Inhaling his breath for what seemed like ages, Terry replied, "Yes."

Being told of what had happened to her, Terry was incensed. How could someone do that to another human being? He thought of his own children, jumping on and off public transport and felt his stomach do cartwheels.

He tried hard to remember the people on his bus that night around that time. The old guy, the girl, a young lad in sportswear, a man in a suit and of course, those giggly girls.

Other people had been on and off the bus, but not at the specific time the officers had asked for.

"You have been most helpful, Mr Walker," said DI Atkins, "anything else should you remember, please ring my mobile." She handed Terry a card. He nodded as he showed them back through the hall and to the front door. "One last thing, what time did you finish your shift on Friday, come Saturday morning?"

"I finished at the depot at about 3am in the morning and arrived home here about 3.30am." he replied.

"Can anyone vouch for that?" continued DS Evans, already halfway up the path.

"The wife," grinned Terry, "never sleeps fully until I'm home."

The police officers shut the gate behind them.

Terry looked at his reflection in the hallway mirror, never in the 13 years he had been a bus driver had something like this happened. Had he driven a rapist to the scene of the crime? Had it been one of those men on his bus?

He shivered and went to start that weeding!

Chapter 14

Back at the station, the entire DI Atkins team was busy working hard; notes and photos had been added to the whiteboard, phones and computers were on and being used.

As DI Atkins and DS Evans entered the room, the noise level quietened and people sat up in their seats.

"Right, what have we got folks?" DI Atkins stood in front of the whiteboard and addressed her team.

"We have just spoke with the driver of the bus that Macy was on; the driver has given us a lot of info, and as much as my gut tells me and with no evidence or proof, I would say he is not a suspect. He has confirmed along with Mike, the landlord of the Admiral Arms, that the people on the bus were probably drinking in the pub that night."

DI Atkins surveyed the room, all eyes on her. Sometimes she almost wanted to be back behind one of the computers, not so on show but she was good at her job and had been headhunted for promotion at the station. She had worked on big cases before and always got results. Word of that had circulated and she had taken the promotion; always being ambitious but never bolchie.

A newly qualified police officer nervously put up her hand. "Susie?" said DI Atkins.

"Er yes, after some research I have discovered that the office party in the pub was from 'Marshall's Insurance' in town. I'm guessing it was someone's birthday or leaving party that night."

"Fab work, Susie, keep it up," smiled DI Atkins. Along with the usual information and slight progress, all seemed to be up to speed with everything.

DI Atkins felt guilty that so many were working at the weekend and not being with their loved ones but unfortunately people didn't always commit crimes just on weekdays and it was the nature of the job.

That's why she had never married or had children; she had had offers but the job had always come first. She had put her own personal life on hold so that she could concentrate on her job and the lives of her victims.

Turning to DS Evans, she said, "I'm gonna finish off paperwork here. You get off, enjoy what's left of the weekend. See you tomorrow 9am sharp, we have Marshall's Insurance to visit."

"OK, boss," answered DS Evans. He didn't need telling twice and grabbed his coat and headed for the exit.

Sunday seemed to drag for Macy, she still ached all over and the sickness in her stomach would not disappear. Lou had been so good, forgoing her own work today in order to look after her, but Macy knew that she couldn't stay here forever and would have to face going back home soon.

The thought though, of seeing the place where she was attacked every time she went out and came home made Macy quiver with fear.

"Shall we go out for a walk? Get some fresh air?" said Lou entering the front room. In all honesty Lou was struggling; she had done the practical thing of getting Macy to the police station but now she felt she had no words to make it better for her friend emotionally. A walk?! How stupid of her! Macy probably wanted to shut herself away indoors, not put herself on show at the local park.

Lou wasn't used to this. In her line of work, she cared for people, made them better and let them go, but Macy wouldn't get better from this. It would always be there for her; no tablet or bandage would make this disappear for Macy. Lou felt so helpless.

To her astonishment though, Macy was pulling on a cardigan. "Yes please, Lou, let's get some fresh air. I keep mulling things over in here, so maybe getting out will make me feel brighter."

Feeling enlightened slightly that she was doing something right to help her friend, Lou fetched her jacket.

Chapter 15

Sorting through paperwork, DI Atkins found what she was looking for; the address for the third party of the person who was with Macy that night – Ritchie Bart.

DI Atkins was unsure whether Macy had been in touch with him since her attack. If she had, he hadn't been in with any extra information that could help them find the attacker, but then he might still be in the dark as to what had happened to his friend after he left her outside the pub that night. Taking her car keys and the address it was time to find out.

Ritchie pulled into the car park of his block of flats and opened the back doors of his van. He had just been to buy a new chest of drawers for his bedroom. Once assembled, the pine three-drawer piece of furniture would look great under his bedroom window.

Lifting the big box out of his van, he locked it and began to walk slowly with it, holding it in front of him to the main door of his flats. Once through the main door, he just had one flight of stairs to climb until he was at his flat. Small beads of sweat began to appear on his forehead and the heaviness of the box was straining his bad leg.

A few more steps, "Come on Ritchie," he said to himself. Unlocking his front door, Ritchie was finally inside. He mopped his forehead with his hand. "Wow, that was heavy."

A quick drink of squash and another round of his painkillers and he would unpack the box and begin the task of reading the instructions and try to assemble the drawers.

Macy walked arm in arm with Lou through the park. She felt better with the sun on her face. They walked slowly, stopping only to look at the blossom on the trees and the flowers in the beds by the lake.

This was just what she needed, she wasn't looking over her shoulder and she didn't feel uneasy, though Macy knew this was due to being with Lou. She felt certain she wouldn't have been able to do this without her.

The girls found a bench and sat down overlooking the serene, peacefulness of the lake. The only noise you could hear was that of the ducks quacking and the faintness of children playing in the play area across the way.

You could forget your problems here, thought Macy, *you could leave your worries behind and just relax*, she closed her eyes.

Lou looked at her friend, and the view. How could some things be so beautiful and other things be so awful? The girls sat for a while in comfortable silence. No words needed to be spoken.

DI Atkins pulled into the car park of Ritchie's flats. She turned off the engine and checked the flat number before getting out of the car.

Ritchie had plastic, wooden pieces, nails and instructions scattered all over his small living room. He had built the shell, now he was tackling the drawers. It was all coming together nicely without too many complications.

His intercom buzzed which made him jump. Strange, he wasn't expecting anyone. He looked at the small screen, no he didn't recognise the lady standing there.

"Hello," said the female voice through the intercom, "I'm DI Atkins and need to speak with you please, Ritchie Bart." Ritchie pressed the button to let the woman in; he felt unnerved. Why on earth would a police officer be knocking on his door? A flutter of thoughts ran through his head as he made his way to the front door.

The woman on the doorstep was smart, of fine stature and quite attractive. She was holding up her identity badge.

"Come in," said Ritchie. "Sorry, the place is a bit of a mess, I've been building a chest of drawers, for my bedroom, its new, I bought it this morning." Realising he was starting to babble out of nervousness, he shut up and instead gestured DI Atkins towards the sofa to sit.

"Ritchie, I've been told you are friends with Macy Reynolds and spent the evening with her on Friday night at the Admiral Arms?"

Macy?? What had Macy got to do with this visit? Ritchie was confused. "Yes that's correct; myself, Macy and Lou."

"Have you spoken to Macy since then?"

"No," replied Ritchie, still unaware of what he was about to be told.

"OK," said DI Atkins, "you may need to sit down then."

Ritchie was numb, he couldn't take in what he had just been told. This wasn't happening, he was hallucinating from his tablets, wasn't he??

Why hadn't he insisted that Macy took a lift with him? He had to see her, or at least speak with her. He tried to recall the events of that evening and what he had done since.

DI Atkins noticed that his hands were clenched together and he was sweating; though to be fair to him, it was hot in the flat and it seemed he was shocked by what she had just told him.

Leaving her card with Ritchie, she saw herself out of the flat. She was glad of the fresh air as his flat had been very stuffy. Walking back to her car, she looked behind her and up at Ritchie's window. She couldn't be sure, but she thought she saw the curtains move. He was watching her.

Ritchie moved away from the window. Should he speak to Macy directly or contact Lou? Did Lou even know herself? Macy may not even pick up, she would be upset, so he rang Lou.

The girls were just returning indoors from their walk; it had done Macy a world of good and she left almost like a normal human being again. Lou's phone rang. She mouthed to Macy, "It's Ritchie," as she answered it.

Macy knew she should have told Ritchie, but saying it out loud made it all so real; telling Harry had been hard enough. She felt bad though, as Ritchie was her friend and she guessed by the phone call now, that he had been visited by the police. Surely he wouldn't hold it against her that he found out second hand?

Lou came out of the kitchen where she had spoken in hushed tones to Ritchie. "He sends his love, Macy, and he said if there is anything he can do, you could call him anytime."

"Aww OK Lou, was he OK? I feel bad that I wasn't the one to tell him," replied Macy.

"He was fine, I think he understands why," nodded Lou.

Ritchie was glad he had spoken with Lou. There wasn't much he could do for Macy but she would now know that he was there for her if she needed him. He surveyed his front room. *Back to assembling these drawers,* he thought.

Chapter 16

Monday morning came with sunshine and just a slight breeze as DI Atkins left for work. She was meeting DS Evans and the others for a quick briefing, then onto Marshall's Insurance to interview the people that were in the pub that night. It would be interesting and she was hoping to have some breakthroughs.

She strode through the main doors and up to the meeting room. Everybody should be refreshed from a few hours off yesterday afternoon and ready for the job in hand.

The room was buzzing, most officers already there, working on the computers or on the phone.

DI Evans quickly followed her into the room. Giving out instructions and tasks to everyone, DI Atkins was satisfied that they were all up to speed on this now.

"Any questions? Any new developments?" she asked. "Yes, guv," said a suited man sitting on the edge of a desk to the right of her, holding a Post-it note in his hand.

"Mike from the Admiral Arms has been in touch again; he remembered the name of the local drinker who was in there that night. A Howard…someone…, doesn't know his surname but thought it might help. Seems to think he is local and always on his own, bit of a loner."

"That's great, will look into that," answered DI Atkins, pulling her car keys from her jacket pocket.

"OK we are off to Marshall's now," she said nodding at DS Evans, "good work everyone, see you later."

The building was enormous, smart and had mirrored glass all around it as DI Atkins and DS Evans walked up to the double doors of Marshall's entrance.

As they entered the hall come foyer, there were plush sofas and small side-tables towards one end, lifts and stairs in front of them and a huge desk where two young girls sat.

Both girls were fashionably dressed, full of make-up and had nails so long that DI Atkins wondered how they ever managed to type or press the keys on a laptop or answer the phone. They would have looked more at home on a catwalk rather than here, behind a desk.

"Good morning," said the blonde girl, "how can I help?" Showing their identity badges made both girls sit up and become more alert. This behaviour made DI Atkins grin inwardly. The power of a badge.

Explaining why they were there and who they needed to see, the brunette girl said, "You need the 12th floor, guys on home/life insurance. I remember it was those lot who went out on Friday, about 12 of them; they left here early for Claire's birthday. I know Claire you see; my older sister went to school with her. I'm friends with her on Facebook too. I saw pics of them all in that pub along the way."

The blonde girl nodded, " I know who you mean, yeah 12th floor you need," she said, flicking her hair about in a flirty way.

"Thank you both for your help," said DS Evans, following DI Atkins to the lift. "I'll buzz up and let them know you are coming," smiled the brunette, obviously glad to have had some gossip to brighten up their day.

Even the lifts were posh in here, spotlessly clean and a female voice telling you what floor you were on every time it moved up. After what seemed like an eternity, the doors opened on floor 12.

Again, they were greeted by another huge desk and this time a young Chinese girl sat behind it. "Good morning, officers," she said politely. "Keeley has just buzzed up. I was expecting you both; the department that you need is the third door down on your right. The manager is Bernard Hathaway and he will be able to answer your inquiries and take you to anybody else you need to speak with."

"You have been most helpful," answered DI Atkins. They made their way down the corridor to the third door down and knocked.

They were greeted by a big burly man, probably in his late fifties. His shirt just about done up and his tie flapped around his middle, not long enough to tuck into his trousers.

DI Atkins observed that his shirt had dark grey buttons on the cuff, not that that ruled him out of course, businessmen had more than one shirt for work but it was something to be noted.

Shaking hands, he ushered them into his office. He didn't recognise the girl in the photo and told the officers that he had spent most of the evening with his back to the rest of the pub, not really noticing much else apart from the people he was with.

He gave the officers the names of the rest of the party there and said they could use his office while they interviewed them. He sent Claire in first.

Chapter 17

Macy felt strange not being at work. She never really did have any time off; only time was when she had a bad bout of flu a few years back.

Harry had been texting her over the weekend and she had given her consent that he could tell the rest of the staff. She wondered if they knew yet. She looked at her watch, 1.21pm. He must have done it by now and she was probably the gossip over the lunch hour. Even though she wasn't even there, she felt herself blushing and feeling ashamed.

Lou had gone to work after much persuasion from Macy at about 10.30am. She was on the day shift so would finish about 7pm. Macy had insisted that she would be fine alone and that she would eat. In fact, Macy had realised that she hadn't moved a muscle since her friend had left. It almost seemed she was glued to the sofa and that if she moved, something bad would happen.

Don't be silly, Macy, she thought and forced herself in to the kitchen. She didn't feel hungry but knew she had to eat something. Macy fumbled about in the fridge and decided on a cheese and pickle sandwich. She would force it down herself if needed and she would sit on the other end of the sofa just to prove a point to herself that she had moved about. There, she felt slightly better already.

Gathering up information that they had been given by several people at Claire's birthday and by Claire herself, DI Atkins felt slightly disheartened. Nothing major had arose or stood out and it seemed that the majority of the party had left before Macy or taken cabs in the opposite direction to Macy's flat. Of course, this would all need to be double checked by the cab company but it all seemed legit according to the home addresses they had been given. She let out a sigh and looking at the list of people on a piece of paper on her lap turned to DS Evans and said, "Should be a bloke called Guy Saunders next."

Guy gently knocked on the door, he had heard snippets about why the police were here but he wasn't completely sure. He just knew they were questioning all those that had drunk in the Admiral Arms Friday night.

"Come in," said a female voice, as Guy turned the door handle. He was greeted by a male and female officer and sat in the chair opposite both of them. He confirmed his name and that he had been in the pub for Claire's birthday. His voice felt shaky and his hands were clenched on his lap. He had never been in a position like this before and he felt completely out of his comfort zone.

DI Atkins observed him and from Macy's description she was almost certain that this was the man Macy had rung her about in the early hours of the morning a few days ago.

DI Atkins explained why they were questioning people in the pub that night and took out the photo of Macy and placed it on the table in front of Guy.

He looked at the photo and thought for an instant that he was going to pass out. It was her, the woman that had caught his eye in the pub and it was her that he had sat behind on the bus.

DI Atkins and DS Evans both glanced at one another; it was obvious that he recognised her and had gone rather pale and ashen looking. His voice was shaking again as he said, "Yes, she was sitting on the other side of the pub from us."

"Did you speak to her at all during the time you were in the pub?"

"No," replied Guy, "our gaze met a couple of times but that was it."

"And this was all you saw of this woman?" continued DI Atkins.

"Er, no," said Guy, "I was on her bus and sat behind her."

Guy was quizzed about the timings of the night and the bus stop and when he had exited the bus. He claimed he had got off at the stop after Macy but could not recall who had left the bus that night with Macy. They would have to verify the timings with his wife of course and with what he had told them seeming plausible, glancing at someone in the pub does not make you a rapist, but why was he sweating and why did he look like he was guilty?

DI Atkins and DS Evans interviewed two more of the people who were there that night, then left telling Mr Hathaway that they could well be back if they had any outstanding inquiries they needed to clear up.

Guy stood at the sink in the men's toilet and stared into the mirror. He looked like he had seen a ghost; pale, white and in shock. He hadn't expected his Monday to start like this. He had told the officers what they needed to know but he had a feeling they would be back for him.

Had that girl remembered him from the pub? Had she felt uneasy with him behind her on the bus? He felt like he was going to explode. Guy turned the tap on and sloshed water over his face, he mustn't show that he was on the edge. Grabbing a tissue to dry himself, he walked back to his desk – upright and confident.

Chapter 18

It was strange at work without Macy, thought Harry as he wandered past her empty desk with a cuppa. She was so reliable, never taking time off unless she really had to. He had already gone over to her desk twice this morning with paperwork for her only to realise upon seeing her empty chair that she wasn't in. His heart sank for her, poor Macy.

With her permission, he had called a staff meeting this morning and without going into too much detail, he had explained why Macy would not be in for a while. He had watched his employees while they digested the information, the smiles on their faces fading and even some welling up, tears in their eyes.

The office had a different feel to it now – quieter and more morose. Not much chatting or laughing going on. One of the older ladies had decided to start a collection and get Macy some flowers. He would hand deliver them to her, thought Harry. He had to see her for himself, give her a hug and tell her everything would be OK.

Back at the station, DS Evans was going through all the 'Howards' in the area. You wouldn't have thought Howard to be a popular name but looking down at the list, this would take him hours.

DI Atkins came through with a pile of paperwork in hand. "I've spoken to the cab firm and all is legit. The times and addresses from everyone at Claire's party all add up."

"Right *O,* Leanne, so that just leaves Guy's story then, right?"

"Exactly, I'm thinking we should visit the wife tomorrow when he is at work and maybe get in touch with the bus driver again. See if he can remember which stop he definitely got off at. Macy feels that she wasn't alone when she left the bus, we just need to find out who got off with her."

"Hmmmmm," replied DS Evans.

"How are you getting on with the 'Howards'?"

"Just eliminating those who are in the wrong age bracket at the moment. Could be here a while," he rolled his eyes.

"Cheese and tomato sandwich?" DI Atkins said as she dropped her paperwork on the desk and headed to the canteen.

Lou found it difficult to concentrate at work today, she was trying to write patients' medicals but her mind kept flitting back to the weekend's events and to Macy. When she had left her, Macy had been curled up on the sofa. A shadow of the independent, outgoing girl Lou knew her as.

She hadn't wanted to keep fussing over her but she would be glad when her shift was over later so she could get back home to her friend.

The afternoon now turning to dusk and DS Evans was still hard at it. The sandwich was all he had eaten today apart from his breakfast this morning. His stomach rumbled.

DI Atkins laughed, "Does that noise mean its home time?"

DS Evans slapped the desk. "Bingo!" he said. "Howard Denver of 94 Primrose Close, must be the man we want as he fits all description and stats."

"OK, let's go question him and then its home time," said DI Atkins already reaching for her coat.

Primrose Close was a funny sort of road. All different houses and bungalows next to each other in the one street. Number 94 was right at the end almost squashed in the corner.

They parked up outside and DI Atkins noticed the front garden was overgrown and all the curtains were closed.

Howard was just washing up his dinner plate when he heard the doorbell ring. He jumped, no one ever came to his door unless it was a delivery driver with a parcel for a neighbour. He quickly dried his hands on a tea-towel and walked slowly to the door. It wasn't a delivery driver because he could see the outline of two figures through the glass panel. Who were they?

As he opened the door, his heart sank. Police officers – this brought back bad memories for him. The man and lady spoke but Howard was not really taking anything in; he showed them into the living room.

It was dark and dingy, thought DI Atkins, could do with a good dust too as her eyes surveyed the dusty mantlepiece. She sat on an armchair which had seen better days and glanced at a newspaper on a trolley beside her open at the crossword page.

Looking around the room, she noticed no family photographs anywhere, Mike at the pub could be right, Howard was a loner. No immediate family, not many friends and certainly not a man who wore a shirt and suit very often.

He looked nervous though, in fact not nervous but frightened almost.

DS Evans started with the questioning and Howard answered very articulately, giving every answer in fine detail. He confirmed he was in the pub that night, that he had sat at the bar and that he had caught the bus home.

When shown the picture of Macy he had said he did not recall her in the pub that evening. It had been very busy but he said a girl was at the bus stop that may have been Macy but he couldn't be 100% certain.

Howard was told to ring a number if he remembered anything else that would help with the investigation.

The officers left after a while and Howard let out a big breath, he felt he hadn't breathed all the time they were there. His body felt like jelly and he had to hold on to the banister to steady himself.

Walking into his kitchen, he poured himself a small whiskey. *Not again*, he thought, *please God not again*.

DI Atkins dropped DS Evans at home and headed back to the station. She should have been going home herself now but something was bothering her.

Perhaps she had seen Howard before, it had made her feel uneasy. Yes, she felt that their paths had crossed sometime in the past.

The bungalow had been eerie, and Howard had been edgy and nervy. Yes, he had answered the questions fully and with no hesitation but she sensed he was holding something back.

She parked her car at the front of the station and headed for the basement where all the old files and records were kept.

Alan was at the desk in front of the door to the basement. He was a retired police officer who just couldn't let go of the job. At 70 years of age, he now kept check on all the old files and helped out current officers with any old crimes they needed to know about.

"Hello, Leanne, what brings you down here?"

"Hi, Alan, this is just a shot in the dark, but have just interviewed a man to do with the Macy Reynolds case and just have this uneasy gut feeling about him, that all isn't what it seems. Tell me, do you know anything at all about a Mr Howard Denver?"

Alan stood rooted to the spot for a moment. God, he hadn't heard that name in years. He was shocked the man was still alive and now after all this time, he was being questioned again, in a case to do with rape.

"I know that name very well, Leanne, I was in charge of the case. Our Howard Denver was accused of raping a woman in 1993, but due to lack of evidence and a good barrister, the jury found him not guilty. All of my working life I have always wondered whether he was innocent or whether he actually got away with it and was free to continue living a normal life. Give me five minutes and I'll get the files."

DI Atkins stood open mouthed, there was definitely something to say about a 'gut reaction' in this job.

Chapter 19

DI Atkins took the files home that night and studied them well into the early hours of the morning.

Howard had been accused of rape by a then 18-year-old girl who had claimed he had assaulted her in the back room of the shop where they both worked. He would have been 44 years old back then, but with just himself and this girl in the room and no witnesses it would have been extremely hard to find him guilty. Her word against his and DNA and technology obviously not so advanced back then, the case would have been open and shut.

They would have to bring him in the following morning and question him further and they would have to find the girl in question, in fact a 43-year-old woman now and make her relive it. If it was true and the woman had been raped by Howard, she had had to live with this and the knowledge he was walking around a free man.

Knowing he may have done it again to someone else could destroy her. DI Atkins shivered, there were parts of this job she hated, she relished catching the criminals and making sure they got punished for their crimes but she always felt for the victims in this job.

They were forgotten about; once a case had been solved, it was file closed and onto the next job, but some victims never got closure.

In bold letters, DI Atkins wrote on a clean sheet of paper: SUSIE LEWIS, one way or another this lady was going to get a shock when they arrived on her doorstep.

Lou arrived home that night to find Macy had cooked dinner and seemed much brighter.

She changed out of her uniform and into comfy Pjs and sat down opposite Macy, looking forward to tucking into sausage and mash. "You look brighter," she said to Macy.

"Yeah, I had a call from DI Atkins earlier, there have been some developments, she couldn't tell me what, but I like her and am confident that she and her team will find whoever did this to me. I can't sit around here moping all day either, so I've decided to go home."

"Are you sure, Macy? You don't have to rush things. You've been through a terrible ordeal," replied Lou in-between mouthfuls of mash.

"I can't stay here forever, and whoever it was, hasn't been in my flat, so I'm safe there. I'll be extra careful as well."

"It's your choice, Macy, but you know you can stay here or be here for as long as you like."

"I know, Lou, but I have to carry on as normal or he would have won, and I can't have that... I need to go back to work as well, I'm soooo bored and keeping myself busy will take my mind off it all."

"Do what you feel is right for you," continued Lou, "you have my support and love, right here 24 hours a day."

"Aww thanks, Lou, you have been a good friend to me through all this, I couldn't have coped without you," replied Macy, getting up and giving her friend a big hug. "What about a glass of wine to toast new beginnings and no looking back?"

"Good idea," said Lou, getting up and pulling open the fridge door to get a bottle.

She felt glad Macy seemed better but she knew Macy still had a lot to go through yet. If they found the man that did this, Macy may have to face him again and she would have this ordeal haunting her, for the rest of her life. Yes, of course she would move on with her life but it would fester at the back of her mind forever, in fact both of them would never forget this for a very long time.

Clinking glasses, Macy sipped at the wine and said, "Anyway enough of me, when is this promotion of yours happening?"

Lou explained she had to see the head of department next week. The girls chatted for ages, drinking the wine and laughing, until night time called and they fell into their beds, probably slightly tipsy but with smiles on their faces.

Chapter 20

Another day, another briefing at the station; though this morning there was much to discuss. Having called DS Evans last night to tell him about Howard, both were in early this morning to go and bring him in.

DI Atkins already had someone on the case to find Susie Lewis, so all was moving along well. She filled everyone in about Howard and answered all the questions.

She still hadn't forgotten about Guy though. His wife needed questioning about timings, so they had a busy day ahead.

First though, Primrose Close, a police car was accompanying them.

Howard saw the police car first through the old, grey net curtains. He hadn't slept a wink last night; he had known this would happen. Detectives were good these days, especially DI Atkins. He had seen her observing his bungalow, gathering ideas and assumptions about him. He knew she would find out about April 1993 when his world had come crashing down around him.

He could not believe this was happening again. He felt sick and weak. Probably the amount of whiskey he had drunk last night to block out the pain didn't help the way he was feeling this morning.

The knock on the door was meaningful and Howard jumped even though he knew they were there. Very slowly, he walked to the door. Why? He had moved away, he had changed his life so that he didn't interfere with anyone, why was this happening again?

It was all a blur to Howard; DI Atkins and DS Evans were speaking, the police took him into the car and before he knew it, he was in a small room opposite the officers, a tape recorder on the table and a cup of water in front of him.

"Susie Lewis," said DI Atkins, "Macy Reynolds – connection please, did you rape these women?"

"No," replied Howard. He could feel himself shaking.

"I don't know Macy Reynolds and have never seen her before; just was in the pub when she was, and Susie Lewis I did not rape, I was cleared of that – not guilty." Howard was angry now. Why was he being used as a scapegoat again? Lots of men were in that pub that night, it could have been anyone of them.

Howard explained that when he worked in the small hardware shop, the boss had employed a young girl, Susie Lewis, to work there with him at weekends. He told the officers that she was a mouthy, ballsy 18-year-old who used to turn up in short skirts and low-cut tops. He told how she thrived on belittling Howard and making cutting remarks towards him.

He had hated the weekends there but needed the money. On the day in question, he relived the hours even the minutes and told the officers every detail. Exactly the same detail he had told the detective back then.

He had shut the shop at 5.30pm, tidied the counter and counted the takings they had made that day. All the while being ridiculed by Susie, for not going out on the 'razz' on a Saturday night, for preferring a night in with the TV. She called him a bore, a freak, a washout.

He said how he had ignored all the insults and pottered on, that she went out into the back room to sort out the nails and screws that needed re-filling in tubs in the shop and heard a clatter. He had gone to the backroom to see what had happened and Susie had dropped all the screws all over the floor.

As he bent to help her pick them up, she had accused him of looking at her cleavage and then with his hands fall of screws, he had misjudged the space between the table and her and had brushed past her, his side touching her bottom briefly.

He then told the officers that she had lost it, saying he would pay for this. The dirty old pervert, trying to rape her. He hadn't touched her, how could he, his hands were full, full of the screws, but he had nobody to back him up, they were alone in the backroom. His word against hers, but thankfully the jury had found him not guilty but he had felt a condemned man ever since and had moved away, had kept himself to himself, never had a relationship, was used to being on his own now. It was easier.

The officer looked at him right in the eye, her eyes softer looking than his.

"Since then, I've never touched a woman again, in fact I've never even smiled at one in case they got the wrong impression."

He had sounded sincere, thought DI Atkins and if he had made this up, he was a very good actor. Still, they did need to hear Susie's side of the story if they could trace her whereabouts, which wouldn't be easy after all these years.

He looked tired and old; would he have been capable of raping Macy Reynolds? DI Atkins didn't know. She switched off the tape recorder and offered Howard a tea. They all needed a break, she reckoned.

She sensed Howard relaxed a little, he unclenched his hands and sat back on his chair. That's how they left him as both officers left the room.

Macy had packed up her things that morning at Lou's and was now outside her flat, bags in hand. She didn't feel as confident now as she had last night but she was still as determined to get on with her life. She had to let the police do their job and she had to carry on too.

She had to admit to herself though, that she had been looking over her shoulder all the while she had walked from her car to her flat and she was almost sure she had closed her eyes when she had walked past the spot where 'it' had happened.

Unlocking the front door, Macy walked into a pile of mail on the floor. Picking it up she continued into her living room. There, all as she had left it, nothing changed, nothing moved. She allowed herself to breathe out. She could do this and she would return to work.

Feeling strong, she unpacked her bags and put the kettle on.

They had no choice but to let Howard go home that afternoon. They had no credible evidence that he was the man they wanted until they heard Susie Lewis' account of events back in 1993, and the bus driver, to make double sure he had got off at Macy's stop.

DI Atkins wasn't so sure now that this was there man; he had given a very detailed account of what had happened with Susie, reliving it as if it were yesterday instead of 25 years ago and he was right that he had never married or had children since. He had withdrawn, almost from society which meant the whole thing had damaged him. Also, he should have got off two stops after Macy, a bus stop being right at the end of his road. He had clarified this but it needed checking.

She could be wrong but she felt he was telling the truth and Mike from the pub was right, Howard was a loner. A sad and lonely old man.

Howard had declined the lift home and had called a taxi instead. He just wanted out of there and rid of the officers questioning and watching his every move.

He had arrived home to find the neighbours twitching the curtains, yes, they had all seen him being manhandled into the police car. That was the trouble nowadays, so quick to judge. Innocent until proven guilty and he was never proven, so they could all poke it.

Still angry about what had happened this morning and clearly shaken about having to open up and hear the name Susie Lewis again, Howard slammed the front door behind him.

The day was far from over for DI Atkins and DS Evans as they headed over to Guy's house to see if his wife was in.

A pretty little thing opened the door of a very nice double fronted detached house.

"Mrs Saunders?" said DI Atkins holding up her ID card.

The lady let them in, her home was neat and tidy but lived in. She led them into the kitchen where two children sat around the table drawing.

"Please sit here," she said pointing to two stools around a breakfast bar. "Tea?"

The officers shook their heads, they weren't here for pleasure. DI Atkins noted that the washing machine was on and there were cute little drawings on the fridge.

"Is this about the poor lady who was attacked? Guy told me all about it. Poor woman," she said in whispered tones so the children didn't hear.

She confirmed everything Guy had told them and their stories pretty much matched up. Where he was, who he was with, whose birthday it was etc.

DI Atkins paused from writing in her notebook. "And what time did your husband get in?" she asked.

"It was about 1am," she answered, "I can never fully get to sleep until he gets in. So when I heard the key in the door, I turned over and glanced at the clock. He also texted me about 11.30pm to say he was about to leave."

The officers glanced at one another. "Could you also tell me what your husband wore that night, please?"

"Tell you, I'll show you!" Guy's wife flung around to the washing machine which had since finished its cycle. She opened the door and pulled out a blue shirt.

"Tada!!" she sang holding it up. "Look I've just washed it, he was also wearing a navy suit but that is at the dry cleaners."

DI Atkins felt the damp, just-washed shirt, looking at both sleeves. She surveyed the cuffs. Both buttons there, plain to see. She sighed. The button of course could be anybody's', in fact it could have been in the grass days before Macy was attacked. Who knows?

"OK, Mrs Saunders, you have been most helpful."

"Not at all," she replied. "I understand you have to eliminate people that were in the pub that night. Glad to be able to assist you."

They nodded goodbye to the children and carried on down the hallway.

"Take care," said Mrs Saunders cheerfully, completely unaware she had just dropped her husband right in it.

Back in the car, DI Atkins and DS Evans looked at one another. "Interesting, he told us he got in at midnight, but she claims it was 1am. What was he doing in that hour? Did he then get off behind Macy at the bus stop? She seemed pretty sure too as she backed it up with the alarm clock statement."

"Exactly," replied DS Evans. "Strange also, that he can't remember who got off at Macy's stop when he can remember everything else that night."

"Very true, have to go back to Marshall's in the morning, bring him in. See what he has to say, though no missing buttons on the cuffs of his shirt."

"No, I clocked that too, Leanne."

They were nearing the station now and DI Atkins' mind pressed on to what else needed doing. Had they traced Susie Lewis yet? Who else from the pub that night did they still need to interview? Did they need to speak with Terry Walker again, the bus driver that night? What had become of any CCTV evidence?

Back at her desk now, she felt tired and exasperated. So many leads but nothing concrete as yet. She needed to phone

Macy. See how she was and to tell her they were following things up.

Macy put down the phone after speaking to DI Atkins, such a lovely lady. She had reassured her they were acting upon all leads they had and things were progressing. Again, Macy had nothing more she could tell her, she hadn't remembered anything else since, nothing that would help them.

She dialled the number for Harry, she couldn't sit-in again twiddling her thumbs and mulling it over, she had to keep busy. It was the best thing and she would be safe in the office, it was all security- manned.

It was lovely to hear Harry's voice, so gentle and caring. He said there was no rush to go back but if she genuinely felt ready, then it was fine with him. Macy placed her phone on the table; right, time to iron something nice to wear to work tomorrow.

Chapter 21

They were all working late at the station, chasing as many leads as they could. The knock on DI Atkins door was assertive and loud. "Come in," she said.

A young male officer opened the door. Smiling, he put a yellow 'Post-it' note on her desk. DI Atkins looked down at it, in large capital letters it read:

FLAT43
COPPELL COURT
ADLEHILL
AD12 9PT

"We traced her Ma'am, its Susie Lewis' address." DI Atkins smiled, a bit of a trek but it was doable in a day.

"Fantastic work, for that you can shut down your computer and go home."

"Thanks," he replied as he shut the door behind him.

Coming out of her office, DI Atkins gathered everyone around and updated them about Susie Lewis and Guy's wife.

"DS Evans and myself will visit Marshall's first thing and bring Guy in. Depending on what he has to tell us will determine how long he is kept here, then we will visit Adlehill to see Susie Lewis. The rest of you, find out all you can about the night in question and keep up the good work, we are all doing really well. Lee, how is the *CCTV* coming along?"

"Slowly, but I'll keep at it. Nothing is springing up at the moment, but it is rather patchy."

"OK, stay on. Right everyone, home time."

Ritchie hadn't heard from Lou or Macy since his last phone call. He had sent the odd text but just received pleasantries back. This probably wasn't a man's domain and Lou was no doubt the best equipped to help and comfort Macy but he did feel a bit left out.

He would ring Macy tomorrow, see how she was doing. He had better not do it now, it was after 9.30pm and he wasn't sure if Macy was still at Lou's.

He got up and made himself a drink and counted out the tablets he had to take before bed. These tablets meant he could have a comfortable night's sleep without his body cramping up. He took them, all in one go. There, done until the next day.

Ritchie went back to the sofa and rested his head on the cushion. He had no recollection of what happened after that, until he woke up the next morning fully clothed on his bed.

The morning brought heavy, black clouds and rain and DI Atkins had to run from her car to the station to avoid getting soaked. She had just hung up her suit jacket to dry a bit when her phone rang. It was a number she didn't recognise, "Hello, DI Atkins."

"Oh, hello," came the response from the other end of the phone. "It's Terry Walker, the bus driver from the night that poor girl was attacked."

"Oh, hi, Terry, how are you?" replied DI Atkins. "I'm fine thanks, it's just that you said to ring you if I remembered anything else and I was driving the bus past the recreation ground yesterday and I recognised the sportswear of the men. One of the men on my bus that night was wearing the same sports jacket. They play for Radcliffe Rovers. Don't know if that information will be of any use to you?"

"That is great, Mr Walker, thank you so much for this news. We will look into this for sure."

"Pleasure officer, goodbye," and the phone line went dead.

Moving into the main incident room, DI Atkins wrote on the whiteboard in big capital letters: RADCLIFFE ROVERS.

Macy breathed heavily as she boarded the train to work. She hadn't felt like having breakfast this morning, so was now feeling slightly peckish. She found a seat and rummaged in her bag for a cereal bar she had in there.

She didn't feel so strong now – being out on her own; she had kept looking behind her to see if she was being followed but as it was rush hour, it was impossible to know. So many people about, rushing here, there and everywhere. Macy outlined everyone on the train. They all looked so normal, no one looked like a rapist, but what were rapists meant to look like anyway?

She realised she had clenched the cereal bar so tight that it had now all crushed into crumbs in the wrapper. Three stops and then a short walk and she would be in the safety of work.

After briefing all her colleagues, DI Atkins and DS Evans headed off to Marshall's. They had both decided to question Guy Saunders in his office and depending what he had to say, then they would decide whether or not to bring him into the station and caution him.

The same two girls sat behind the big desk in the main reception.

The brunette, fluttering her eyelashes at DS Evans and looking only at him said, "Good morning, officers, how are you both?"

Not in the mood for pleasantries today, DI Atkins who just wanted to get on with the job replied, "We know where to go thanks, so we'll just head up there."

Raising her eyebrows and rolling her eyes the brunette said, "OK then, fine."

Guy was just typing an email when the door to his office opened. He gasped a little when he saw the two officers standing there.

"Good morning, Mr Saunders, we are here to ask you a few more questions, as having had already spoken with your wife, there are a few discrepancies we need to clear up," DI Atkins voice was stern and assertive.

Guy beckoned them to the chairs in front of his desk. "Er yes, my wife did say that you had spoken with her." He realised he had not moved his hands from the keyboard and his screen had since shut down. Wiping the sweat away from his brow, he said quietly, "How can I help you some more?"

"You claim to have got in an hour before your wife says you did; can you account for that hour please? What did you do? Where did you go? Did you follow Macy and attack her?" DI Atkins felt irate now.

"No, no!" stuttered Guy back. "I did not attack that girl."

"Then where were you from midnight till 1 am when you then arrived home?" DI Atkins slapped the desk making the pens and computer mouse shudder.

"OK, OK, I was with Claire." There was silence.

Guy inhaled a deep breath and carried on, "Claire and I are having an affair. We left the pub, I got the bus, she made her way home in a cab. I did text my wife saying I was on the way home, then Claire started texting me, saying for me to get off the bus and go to hers. So, I did, which meant that was why I was late home. I didn't say anything before because I didn't know you were going to speak to my wife and I didn't want to drop Claire in it either."

Neither DI Atkins or DS Evans had quite expected this revelation.

DS Evans spoke first, "OK Mr Saunders, we will have to speak to Claire separately, to see if she verifies this."

"She will," continued Guy, "just please don't tell my wife."

"Your extramarital affairs have nothing to do with us," said DI Atkins, "we are only here to find out who attacked Macy Reynolds, but be warned Mr Saunders, you are playing a dangerous game and for all your lies, you will get found out."

Guy hung his head, he knew it was wrong, but life was so dull at home, almost habit formed now. With Claire, it spiced life up a bit and was exciting, thrilling even, catching that odd moment together at work with no one else knowing was exhilarating.

He breathed out, glad he had finally confessed the truth, so he was no longer a suspect and glad, he had to admit, that the officers were probably not going to tell his wife.

DS Evans stayed with him whilst DI Atkins went to find Claire. She was outside, having five minutes fresh air on one of the balconies when DI Atkins found her. Claire knew straight away why she was there. She confirmed to the officer that Guy was telling the truth. That he had got off the bus, headed to hers that night and then left in time to be home at 1 am.

It all added up, thought DI Atkins, her address was on the bus route and the time she said Guy had left would have given him time to get from hers to his by 1 am.

DI Atkins looked at Claire; she was attractive, though not as attractive as Guy's wife, how does a woman get herself involved with a married man with two kids? What was the attraction when she could quite easily get herself a single man? Was it the thrill, the chase, the excitement? Who knew? People did funny things when they thought they were in love.

She made her way back to DS Evans. "OK, let's go, we are done here. Thank you for your co-operation, Mr Saunders." With that the door slammed behind them.

Macy had made it to work, although feeling jumpy all the way, until she had walked through the big double doors. She had made it!

Now walking down the corridor to her desk, she felt emotional, trying to control herself; Harry came out of his office. "Macy, oh Macy," he said meeting her with the broadest of smiles and biggest of hugs.

Harry's hugs were safe, Macy thought. "How are you doing, my lovely, you sure you are ready for coming back to work?"

"Harry, I've got to get on with my life or he would have won," replied Macy. Through her words the tears came and Harry hugged her once again.

"Come on," he said, "let's get you to your desk and I'll put the kettle on. You don't have to start work just yet!" he winked.

Macy got to her desk where she was greeted by the most beautiful bouquet of flowers; pink, white and yellow. She cried some more when she read the card and all the lovely, supportive comments from her work colleagues. A few rallied round her desk, also hugging her and speaking words of comfort and encouragement and finally Harry did make that cup of tea!

Ritchie had a break in his deliveries and pulled out his phone. Finding Macy's contact he started to type out a message. Hovering over the buttons he struggled to find the right words. Looking at the screen he had only managed:

HI MACY, HOW ARE YOU?

What next? What do you write to someone who has recently been raped? As feeble as it was, he ended his message with:

THINKING OF YOU, SPK SOON, R XX

There, sent, he put his phone back in his pocket. He had always liked Macy, she was fit and attractive and he had always wondered if he had a chance with her, but he had never got any vibes back and felt that if anything happened between them, that it would upset the threesome of their friendships, so he had settled with just being a friend.

After grabbing a quick sandwich, DI Atkins and DS Evans were now on their way to question Susie Lewis. Having drawn a blank with Guy Saunders, DI Atkins felt frustrated that all their leads were leading nowhere. Still, let's see what this Susie had to say.

After what seemed like ages, they arrived in Adlehill; a built-up sort of town. *Lots of tower blocks and small news agent shops,* thought DI Atkins. Not much greenery but lots of grey and hazy air.

Turning the corner, they turned up opposite Coppell Court. A big tower block, comprising about 15 floors, guessed DI Atkins.

"I hope my car is safe here," quirked DS Evans observing the small gang of youths across the way.

"Hmmmmm," answered DI Atkins, thinking the area didn't look very safe at all. Cars with their windows smashed in, glass over the pavements and litter spilling out of the bins. A very desirable area!

"The old bill are here, spit on them!" shouted a youth cycling up on a bike.

DI Atkins always wondered how people knew they were the police, especially as they were plain clothed. It was like they had it tattooed across their foreheads.

"Spit on them? I wouldn't waste my saliva," gobbed another youth, screeching up near them on a silver BMX. The rest of the gang laughed. Clearly the gang leader, the boy on the BMX said, "we don't grass here on Coppell Court so whatever you're looking for, you won't get no answers."

He was now in front of DI Atkins. "On your way now, please," she said as she walked around him and into the ground floor of the flats.

It smelt of urine and the lift smelt even worse, but it was better than taking the stairs as number 43 was on the 14th floor. The lift was rickety and old, a bit like the block of flats. DI Atkins wondered if it would even reach level 14, she didn't fancy being stuck in this for hours, that was for sure.

The light in the lift went green and the doors opened to the 14th floor. Phew! They had made it.

Number 43 was to the left of the lift, a brown heavy door with gold numbers on it and a small knocker. DS Evans knocked. They stood for a while before a lady, in a small denim skirt, white vest top(her ample bosom hanging over the top of it), and a cigarette in her mouth opened the door. "Yeah," she said in a most unfriendly manner.

"Susie Lewis?" DI Atkins said.

"Who wants to know?"

Holding up their ID cards, the officers both replied at the same time, "We do."

"What's he done now? Look, whatever it is, it ain't my fault, I can't keep tracks on him all the time, not with two other little kids to keep my eye on."

Still on the door step, DI Atkins guessed she may have been referring to the youths downstairs.

"No, we are here to see you. Ms Lewis, no one is in trouble. We need to speak to you about a Mr Howard Denver." She saw the eyes change in the woman and if she had been a tiny bit slower, the officers would have had the door shut in their faces, but DI Atkins had seen it happening and had wedged her foot just in time in-between the door and the step.

"I don't wanna talk about him," said Susie, "for fucks sake Kiana, keep the noise down!" She had turned her head back in towards her flat and referred to the noise coming from a child in there.

"I know it must be hard for you," continued DI Atkins, "to relive something that happened in your past but it is important to us, it will help us follow an inquiry we have ongoing at the moment."

Reluctantly, Susie stepped back from the door, "You had better come in then."

It was a haze of smoke as they walked in and it smelt of tobacco too. There were toys everywhere and just a general feel of messiness and poverty. A ripped sofa greeted them in the small front room and two small faces turned to look at them.

"Kiana, take Skye into the bedroom and keep her occupied for a while," told Susie to what looked like a four-year-old. She scooped up the baby and went into one of the two bedrooms.

Inhaling smoke from the cigarette she had had in her mouth since opening the door, Susie said, "What's all this about then?"

The officers explained why they were there and that Howard was one of the suspects in the inquiry. They wanted to know exactly what had happened to her back in 1993.

Susie stuttered and nodded after hearing this, lighting up another cigarette and looking DI Atkins right in the eye, she said, "Howard Denver didn't rape that girl, he doesn't have it in him, and he didn't touch me up either, back then in the shop. I made the whole thing up."

"OK," replied DI Atkins, stunned at the statement she had just heard. "Why?"

Susie looked down, more subdued now and not as bold. "I was with this guy, he needed money, so we hatched this plan. If I said Howard had raped me, I could get media money, compo money etc. and it was easy, it was only us two in the shop most of the time."

She continued, "Instead, it backfired, went too far and he got found not-guilty. I got nothing, just a beating from the boyfriend for all my troubles. Huh! We split up soon after."

DI Atkins and DS Evans looked at one another, Howard had been telling the truth. Deep down they had both known that but they had to follow it up. DI Atkins made a mental note to tell Alan the outcome of this visit. He would be interested particularly as he had headed this case all those years ago.

"Will I get into trouble now? As I can't leave me kids, got no one that will take these lot in," Susie waved her arms in the air.

After all these years, it really was not worth dragging it all up again, thought DI Atkins but she would tell Howard that Susie had finally admitted she had made the whole thing up. He was entitled to that, at least.

"No Susie, we will not be taking it further, but we are grateful that you have finally been honest and helped us at least with this present investigation." The officers both got up to leave, Susie breathed a sigh of relief.

"Still, I'm sure he got over it, the gullible old sod, always was an easy target," laughed Susie.

DI Atkins turned to her, she thought of Howard, lonely in his house, tormented and pained by this sad, sorry affair.

"Actually, he never got over it, Susie, what you did to him has tormented him ever since. He has never got married, had children; in fact, probably not even so much as spoke to a woman in that sense since! He lives alone like a recluse all because of what you made up! So, no, we won't take it any further but you can be rest assured that you can now live with the fact that you ruined a perfectly decent man's life!"

With that, DI Atkins left the flat and pressed the down button on the lift, closely followed by DS Evans, leaving Susie for once in her life completely speechless.

Chapter 22

Macy switched her computer off. She had made it through her first day back at work. She sat back on her chair and felt elated, normal even and for most part of the day, she had almost forgotten what had happened to her.

She pulled her phone out of her bag; she had been so busy today, catching up with everything and everyone that she had had no time to look at it. She had the usual emails and a text from Ritchie. Clicking on it, she wished upon anything that she had taken him up on the offer of a lift home that Friday. If she had only got into his van, none of this sorry mess would have happened.

Quickly replying that she was OK and had completed her day back at work, she looked at her watch. Phone back in bag, a quick tidy of her desk and she would be off. Though the thought of getting on that packed train panicked her. She looked out of the window, all those people out there, it could be any one of those, he could be waiting for her, outside or at the station or even by her flat.

"You OK, Macy?" said Harry walking into her office. Macy jumped, "Oh Harry, you frightened me."

Realising she was nervy, Harry apologised, "Sorry Macy, my fault for creeping up on you."

"I was daydreaming that he was out there, waiting for me. In here, I feel safe but out there…" she went quiet.

"Look," said Harry, "I'm going to leave in five minutes, I'll give you a lift home, it's no bother and I would feel better if I knew you were home safe and sound."

"Oh, Harry, it's out of your way, I'll be fine."

"No buts, Macy, just accept that is what's happening."

She went to protest again but not accepting Ritchie's lift had got her into this, so maybe she just had to accept people cared for her.

At the station, DI Atkins stared at the big whiteboard. She stared at Guy Saunders' picture and Howard Denver's picture and all the lines of enquiry leading from it. If they hadn't attacked Macy, then who did?

She was even getting her colleagues to look at similar cases, in case they had a serial rapist on the loose.

She took the board rubber and erased all the information about Guy and Howard and then removed their photos from the board. She looked at both their photos – both innocent, both had proven that in more ways than one.

Next port of call, following up Terry Walker's phone call about the footballer from Radcliffe Rovers. She had looked online and saw they trained tomorrow evening, so that was her and DS Evans' job tomorrow night. Maybe something would come from that but right now they were drawing blanks and she didn't like that.

Chapter 23

Harry and Macy were almost at her flat. They had chatted all the way home about nothing in particular, but it had made Macy feel much calmer. "There you go," said Harry as he pulled into one of the visitor parking spaces.

"Thanks so much, Harry, I'm so grateful. I'm not sure how I would have managed on the train with these lovely flowers."

"Not a problem, I'll walk you to the main doors."

"Don't be silly, Harry, I'll be fine from here," but Harry gave her such a look that Macy protested no more.

Walking along the path, Harry said, "Beryl said come for dinner, this week or next. You choose which evening, weekday or weekend. Up to you."

"Aww, Harry, that's so kind, thank Beryl for me won't you. I'll let you know a day soon."

By now, they had reached the main doors to Macy's flat. Harry pecked her on the cheek. "Well done for today, Macy, I'm proud of you. See you tomorrow."

Macy felt her eyes well up. "I won't let the bugger win," she said.

"That's my girl."

Macy went inside and unlocked the door to her flat. Dinner, a glass of wine and a chat with Lou, then bed, ready to do it all again tomorrow, feeling even more stronger than today, she hoped.

DI Atkins made her way down the corridor to see Alan. Having satisfaction that a case could really be closed, dealt with, gone, meant a lot to the officers. A lot of them lived with the 'not knowing', had the decision gone the right way? Guilty or not guilty?

Having evidence was one thing, but you were not at the crime when it was happening, arriving always just after, wasn't always enough to know exactly what happened.

Now Alan would have concrete knowledge, to know exactly what went on, that Susie had at last told the truth and the 'not guilty' verdict to Howard all those years ago was the correct judgement.

"Hey, Alan," she said finding him knee deep in boxes.

"Oh, hi, Leanne, how's things? Excuse the mess, just having the annual tidy up of all the old cases. Adding new ones, moving around old ones. I like them in alphabetical order."

She grinned, Alan had always been methodical and meticulous. "We visited Susie Lewis."

Alan stopped what he was doing. "Go on."

"She admitted that she made the whole thing up for money. Howard never raped her, she said so herself."

DI Atkins could have sworn she just physically saw the stress leave Alan's body. He looked lighter almost, as if the weight of that case had just lifted from him.

"Except the whole thing backfired on her because he was found, rightly so, not guilty. Left her with no relationship and definitely no money."

Alan was silent for a while, until whispering, "Poor man, she ruined his life. For what?"

"Greed, Alan, pure greed," she replied.

Chapter 24

Ritchie was bored; he was sat at home, having taken his medication, had his dinner and now was staring at the TV, having really no idea what he was watching.

He twiddled with the label on his T shirt. He would *go* for a drive, that would relieve the boredom.

Ritchie got up and went to find his van keys. He hadn't thought where he would drive to, he would just drive and see where he ended up. Probably a pub somewhere, have a coke.

He locked his front door and jumped in his van. Driving relaxed him, like it did when he could go out on his motorbike. He would drive for miles, forgetting all the stresses of the day, all his worries. The air blowing around him, feeling free, feeling alive. Being in the van didn't quite have the same effect, but it did relax him.

He drove for some time, past shops, past fields, past houses. He was just turning left into a side road when a woman on the street caught his eye. Her long brown hair swayed in the gentle breeze and her petite little figure was easy on the eye.

Macy! It was Macy! What was she doing out here on her own?

Ritchie wound the window down and said, "Hey, Macy."

The girl turned her head slightly but carried on walking. He turned the wheels of his van, so it was nearer the kerb and slowed down.

The girl quickened her step. "Macy, it's me Ritchie."

Still the girl did not look at him. Why was Macy ignoring him?

Feeling agitated, Ritchie stopped the van and got out. Running towards the girl, he shouted out her name again. Still, she did not look behind her.

He was right behind her now and he grabbed her arm. The girl froze, his grip was tight around her. "Macy, why are you not answering me?"

His saliva splashed in her face, where he was so rushed and aggravated. "Let...go...of...me...I'm not this Macy."

By now, he had pushed her into the fence, his body right up against hers, still gripping her arm. The girl was shaking and she felt that at any given moment her legs would buckle beneath her.

She let out a scream. A loud frightful scream. Ritchie jolted back; the girl noticed the emptiness in his eyes.

"Leave me alone, I'm not the girl you are looking for." She ran then, she ran for her life, looking back to see if he was following her. She ran all the way home.

Ritchie wretched into the kerb. What had just happened? He blinked his eyes; it was all a blur. What was he doing here? He really didn't know where he was. He saw his van up the road and began to walk to it. Why did that girl scream? He had just been walking behind her, hadn't he?

Climbing into his van, he reached for the bottle of water in the side compartment and drank it all down in one go. *Home now*, he thought, still feeling slightly dazed.

Chapter 25

Having enjoyed a full and long good night's sleep, DI Atkins was ready to take on the day. Lots of paperwork to do at the station and then tonight to find the man from the football team who was on the same bus as Macy that fateful night.

She had already briefed everyone, though not much had developed unfortunately but everybody was busy on different things.

Macy too, had had a good night's sleep, probably the first one in what seemed like ages. She hadn't woken up sweating and clutching the covers, nor had she had any nightmares, with which she felt grateful for.

Macy was at her desk now, feeling in control of her emotions and ready to start work. She had to admit though, that she still felt shaky and vulnerable getting to work and had breathed a sigh of relief when she had entered her workplace, but still, she was here now and safe.

Katie Smith, however, hadn't slept a wink, she had run all the way home and had nearly collapsed once she had gotten through her front door. Her feet black and blistered from running and her whole body shaking. Christ, what had happened last night?

She had been up and down all night trying to figure it all out. Had the guy been drunk? Had she just escaped being kidnapped? Or had it just been a case of mistaken identity? Her head hurt; she was so confused.

There was no way she could work today. Being a primary school teacher, she had to be on the ball and there was no chance that she could stand up in front of a class of 30 six-year-olds and teach. She had already phoned in and said she had a bug, which meant she could be off tomorrow as well. The 48-hour rule!

She might as well have had a bug, she felt so sick. Looking in the mirror, she still couldn't quite believe it. Seeing the man's face as clear as day in her mind, she couldn't work it out. It was like he had known what he was doing but then again didn't.

She sloshed water over her face, as if doing that would erase the picture of him in her mind. As a teacher's work was never done, she would do some marking and then plan the DT day that was coming up. She needed to keep busy.

Chapter 26

The station was buzzing. Phones ringing, voices talking, computers and printers beeping.

DI Atkins sometimes couldn't stand all the noise and hustle and bustle of it all, but she knew it meant everyone was busy which was a good thing, but sometimes it all got too much especially when she needed to think about stuff and find answers to the things mulling around in her head. She needed to get out, away from it all.

She beckoned DS Evans over, who was taking a break from the computer screen and sipping tea. Walking over with his mug, he said, "Yes, Leanne, you OK?"

"Yeah, I am, but just need an hour away from all this. I'm gonna head over to Howard Denver's place, tell him about Susie's confession."

"OK, guv, do you want me to come with you?"

"No, I'll be fine. Make sure everyone takes a lunch break please."

"Right, will do. Give the poor fella my regards won't you."

"I will," DI Atkins replied.

Just as she was heading out to the front desk and the automatic doors, she turned to see a familiar, annoying face at the desk. She sighed; how did the press always find out? Bloody social media and all that, she supposed.

She knew Matthew Simmons well and knew he was just trying to do his job and make a living like everyone else but he was just so irritating. He worked for the local newspaper and always, always seemed to have a knack at knowing what was going down.

With his rucksack on his back and papers rustling in his hands, she walked over to him. The policeman behind the desk grinned at her, thankful she was there so that he could escape him.

"Well, well, well Matthew Simmons, how lovely to see you here," she said sarcastically.

Both having a love/hate relationship, he answered, "Just doing my job, missy, the same as you do yours!"

She ushered him into a side room. He was talking before she could even shut the door. With his round, silver glasses, small blue eyes, balding hairline and geeky clothes, he would have been much better suited to train-spotting, she thought.

"Rumour has it that a local girl has been raped, how close are you to finding the man who did it and is he a serial rapist or a murderer even?"

Why was it that journalists always liked to exaggerate the truth times ten. She guessed that's what made the headlines and why people bought the newspapers.

"Come and sit down, Matthew, now how have you come to find this out?"

"Talk of the street, miss."

Now she knew this was not exactly true but she did know that it only took one snippet of information or one overheard private conversation for stuff like this to leak out.

"You're getting way ahead of yourself, Matthew, just slow yourself down."

He had already taken out a pen and paper and was vigorously writing down everything she was saying. It was catch 22 really; if she denied it, he would just make it up which she didn't want and if she gave away too much information, it could jeopardise the case. Either way it was going to make the local paper, she just had to be careful what information she divulged and just hope he didn't add bits on or exaggerate it too much.

"A girl was attacked last week and we are following all lines of enquiries. That's all I have to say on the matter now."

Matthew punched the lid on his biro. Seriously, she could be hard work. One bloody sentence about it, how could he write a frontpage piece with just that!

"Come on, DI Atkins, a bit more information please. Where did the attack happen? Who is in the frame? Who is the girl?"

"Nope, Matthew, nothing more," said DI Atkins getting up, "the girl has the right to remain anonymous."

She opened the door for him to leave. Packing up his stuff into his rucksack, he said, "You are a hard one to crack, you know."

"Come on, Matthew, that's old news!" she winked.

Making sure, she watched him go through the doors, she headed for her car. *Now for Howard Denver*, she thought, who would be slightly easier to manage than Matthew Simmons.

She drove into Primrose Close and parked just a way down from Howard's. She needed to phone Macy first, tell her the press has got wind of her story. She dialled Macy's number. She hated these phone calls, the phone calls where she had no real news of the case progressing but news that everyone was to know something bad had happened locally and Macy was the victim, bang in the thick of it. Though she would emphasize that no names had been mentioned and she would be positive with Macy that this could be a good thing with it going in the paper. It could jog somebody's memory, or the attacker himself may come forward. They could get new leads from it.

Macy stood by the window in the office, it was like time had stood still for a minute. She had just come off the phone to DI Atkins. It wasn't her fault, Macy knew that, but just as she was starting to feel less of a wreck and the physical pain was fading, she was delivered another blow.

The media knew! A story to be printed in the local paper. What if they did have her name? Everybody would know, she would be stared at in the street, whispered about behind her back. Known as Macy Reynolds, the girl who was raped.

She felt sick, who had leaked it? As DI Atkins had said, it was probably not done on purpose. An overheard conversation or a snippet of something that the press had dug a bit deeper for.

True, it could open up new enquiries, DI Atkins had stressed that but even so, this nightmare was continuing and Macy felt lost, not in control of anything anymore. She hoped and prayed they just didn't print her name.

"Tea Macy...Macy?" She was brought out of her bubble of thought by Jennifer, one of the office juniors, holding out a mug of tea for her.

"Oh er…Thanks, Jen," Macy said as she reached for the mug.

"You OK? You look like you have seen a ghost."

"Yeah, I'm OK," replied Macy. *A ghost, yeah almost*, she thought, as this whole situation was becoming more and more surreal.

Putting her phone back in her bag, glad that the phone call was over, DI Atkins walked towards Howard's. She was glad she was able to have some better news for a change. Though, now that he had lived his life for all those years after the incident, it wouldn't be much of a consolation. She knocked on the door and waited a while until he came to open it.

"Hello, Mr Denver," she said only half raising her ID card as he knew who she was by now. "OK to come in?"

He stood aside so she could enter. He looked nervy and frightened. Hoping that she sounded reassuring she said, "Howard, I've come with some news that I hope will be of some comfort to you."

Now sitting next to him on the old, torn and worn sofa, she placed her hand on his which was rested on his knee.

"We found Susie Lewis and questioned her about the allegations she made against you and she finally admitted that she made the whole thing up, all of it lies."

DI Atkins felt Howard's body relax, his hand gripping hers. Turning his lowered head to face hers, his sad eyes slightly brighter now, he said, "I never thought this day would ever come. I knew I was innocent, that I never touched her. The courts knew I was innocent but as soon as you are tarred with something like this, people always judge you. I knew I'd never be free until she admitted it."

"You are free now, Howard, she didn't benefit from it at all, in fact she lost from it. She was young, naive and stupid and I really hope she has learnt from her mistake."

"Why did she do it? Did she tell you that?"

DI Atkins looked at him, "Love and greed, Howard."

His head now in his hands, Howard sobbed, releasing all the tension and heartache that he had held for so long.

DI Atkins sat with him in silence until the sobbing ceased and he sat back. She could almost see the tension had gone in his face, some lines and wrinkles almost disappearing.

"Thank you, thank you," he said over and over.

DI Atkins got up and said, "I'm glad I could bring closure for you. Thank you for your help with the present case and now I hope that you can move on," she stretched out her arm, "stay there, I'll see myself out."

He sat, "I hope you get him, you know. I hope you get the man that did that to that poor young girl."

"I will," shouted DI Atkins as she closed his front door behind her.

She didn't go straight back to the station, instead she drove to a cafe. She sat and ordered a tea and a bacon sandwich and sat by the window. She watched the passers-by, all busy with their lives. She mulled everything over – the suspects that were now not suspects, Macy, what the newspaper would say tomorrow and a niggling little thing that had been bothering her for a while now. It was a known fact that in most, though not all cases, the person knew their attacker.

Was it somebody that Macy knew, she would find out, that was for sure. Finishing her sandwich and slurping the last sip of tea, the 'DI Atkins me time' had finished.

Chapter 27

The hospital was packed, no bed left vacant. Lou was almost glad she was on earlies this week. She looked at her watch, one hour to go, then clocking off time. If she got out on time, it would be just after 3pm. She could pop to the shops, then head home to make a start on revising and thinking about her interview that was coming up. She wanted this promotion, she loved her career and wanted to do well in it.

Pushing the trolley with all the medication on it, she went into the ward to do her last medicine batch of the shift. A lovely smile on her face and a sympathetic ear certainly helped in this job.

Billy finished work and headed home. Training tonight which meant an easy, quick dinner, a quick change into the kit and a short drive to the recreation ground. He loved getting together with the lads, playing a sport he so enjoyed.

DI Atkins and DS Evans were also getting ready to head down to the recreation ground. Since returning to the station she had felt more refreshed and revitalised after spending some time alone and had completed lots of the necessary paperwork.

The CCTV was almost finalised and they should get some answers back from that tomorrow, once analysed again. It was a tedious job, going over hours and hours of CCTV, but vital in their line of work.

DS Evans unlocked his car and DI Atkins slid into the passenger seat. His turn to drive tonight.

When they arrived, she could see the team practising on the other side of the field. She could hear shouts of praise, their names and also cheers. Could one of these men here be responsible for Macy's attack?

They walked towards the players. Some men hesitated in their play, slightly unnerved that two strangers were on the side-lines watching them training.

A man came up to them, puffing, out of breath. "Hey guys, all OK here?" he held out his hand to DS Evans, "I'm Robbie, the club captain, you're not footy scouts, are you? Premiership here we come!" he chuckled as he spoke, though the grin faded when the pair held up their identity cards.

The whole team had come closer by now, intrigued to know what was happening.

"It has been brought to our attention that some or most of you were drinking in the Admiral Arms pub last Friday," said DI Atkins.

"Yeah, that's right, we went after our training session," replied Robbie. "Why, has someone complained that we were too rowdy?" he laughed nervously; somehow, he felt this was quite serious.

"We need to know which one of you left there and stood at the bus stop opposite the pub and journeyed on the bus home, please?"

111

A small but stocky man came forward. "I think you're looking for me then," he said, "Billy Tomlin."

DS Evans escorted him away from the group with DI Atkins closely behind, to the nearest bench in the park. "Do you remember this woman?" DI Atkins showed him the photo of Macy.

Billy studied it and after what seemed like a long while, he answered, "Yes I do, can't say for sure if she was in the pub, but she was at the bus stop and got on the same bus as me."

"OK, can you remember if she got off at the same stop as you?"

Billy closed his eyes as if that would make him remember more, "I think she did, but I was pretty drunk so can't be 100%, why?"

"Because, Mr Tomlin, on that night this woman was followed, raped, attacked and left by her flat."

Billy wasn't expecting that reply and fell quiet, he tried really hard to remember anything else that could help the police, then it dawned on him, could they be here talking to him because they thought it could have been him?

"Look, it wasn't me, I only just managed to get myself home, let alone follow and…" he couldn't even say the words, finish the sentence, he felt sick.

"Did anyone else get off the bus at that time too?" said DS Evans.

Billy thought hard, "Maybe," he said, "but I cannot be certain. I got off the bus, walked a bit then crossed the road to my turning and I'm sure she carried on walking, but it was dark and I was drunk."

Confirming his address, this would add up thought DI Atkins. "OK, thank you for your help on this matter." They got up to leave.

Billy got up too and something clicked in his brain, it was probably nothing but all the same it was worth mentioning. "Hold on," he said. The officers turned to look at him. "It might be nothing but I remember when crossing the road, a vehicle was coming at me quite fast, headlights beaming brightly, I could barely see. I had to virtually run halfway across the road."

"Right," said DI Atkins, "can you recall what sort of vehicle it was?"

"It was hard to make out because of the headlights but I would say a van or land rover type."

"Thank you."

As the officers began to walk across the grass, Billy called after them, "I hope the girl is OK, through my drunken haze, I remember she had a kind face."

They nodded and continued to walk, leaving Billy to fill in his bemused teammates. "Telling the truth?" said DS Evans to DI Atkins.

"Yeah, I think so," she replied as she mentally crossed his name off the suspect list.

Chapter 28

Macy didn't sleep that night, tossing and turning continually. She was so worried about what the paper would say in the morning.

She had spoken to Harry at work and he had reassured her that as long as her name wasn't mentioned, it would all be OK. It would still just be her friends that knew. She knew he was right and DI Atkins had specifically told her she hadn't given her name, but still she felt unsettled. To see it printed out in black and white and to know people were reading and talking about her made her stomach churn.

Harry had offered her the day off but she needed to keep busy, keep her mind occupied, so she got out of bed and got herself ready to face another tough and difficult day.

Guy was the first in the office this morning which was unlike him, but with the aftermath of the situation, he felt being at work at the moment was slightly better than being at home.

He hadn't told his wife about Claire; he felt there was no point in distressing her, especially as himself and Claire had both decided to call time on their fling. Both agreeing that they both had too much to lose with continuing it. Things had been a bit awkward in the office but it was getting better. They tried not to see too much of each other and made a special effort not to be left alone together.

Thinking that he would feel better for this, that he was not having to lie anymore, not having to skulk around, not having to cover his tracks, but in fact he felt worse. In truth, he had liked Claire, grown to care for her and he had felt flattered that she had liked him. It had been exciting, frantic at times, thrilling and he had enjoyed that. Their little secret, but in reality it was wrong. He was married and a father and yes, what sort of role model was he for his kids, going about sleeping with someone else.

The trouble was, now that the affair had finished, he felt flat, back to the usual routine and habits, nothing to exhilarate him anymore.

He had to try harder with his wife; bring some spark back into their relationship, but it was hard after many years of marriage. Things went stale.

He let out a big sigh and looked around the office, still no sign of anyone yet. He pulled the local newspaper out of his briefcase. Just ten more minutes, then he would turn his laptop on and start work.

Guy leaned back on his chair and unfolded the paper. He stared at the front cover. In big black bold lettering, he read:

LOCAL GIRL RAPED AND ATTACKED OUTSIDE HER HOME.

He carried on reading and knew the article was about the girl he had been questioned about. His stomach churned, it seemed the police had not caught anybody yet and whoever it was, was still roaming free.

He still couldn't quite believe he had been caught up in all of this and that the police had once suspected him. He shuddered and wondered if this horrible act had never happened to the girl that night, or if his own evening had panned out differently, whether he and Claire would still be seeing each other. His thoughts were interrupted as the phone started to ring and his colleagues begun to turn up for work.

Katie sat in the staff room, trying to make sense of what she was reading. The caretaker always bought and left the local newspaper in the staff room for all to read.

Hardly ever being one of those people who did, today Katie had felt drawn to it and now she knew why. A local girl had been raped and left it seemed for dead. Could this have any connection to what had happened to her two evenings ago?

She knew she had to go to the police with this information, even if it wasn't connected, she somehow needed to say out loud what had happened to her. Katie hadn't told a soul but was still plagued and shaken up by the frightful event and didn't she owe it to this girl to do something if this wasn't just a coincidence?

She would go to the police station after school today. She placed the paper back down on the table. Aware that she wasn't behaving like her normal self, she tried to put this to the back of her mind until later. Katie straightened her skirt, forced a smile on her face and went to meet her class. She had a full day of teaching to get through.

Howard Denver locked the door behind him; for once in a long, long while, he walked down the street, not with his head hanging down facing the pavement but up high.

He even felt he had a skip to his step. It felt like he was walking on air!

He was going to the newsagents to collect the local paper like he had done for many years but today it felt like it was the first time he had done it as a free man.

However, once Howard had got to the newsagents and glanced at the headlines, he didn't feel so upbeat anymore. He felt saddened to read about the young girl and even more so, ashamed that he was connected with it. He had to realise though that it was just circumstantial that he had been in the same pub and then on the same bus and that was as far as it had gone.

Walking back, desperate now to get back home, he had to believe he was an innocent man, but it was so hard to shake off the stigma that he had lived with for many years.

It didn't take him long to get back home and once inside, he read and re-read the article until he could take it no more and ripped up the whole paper and threw it around the room.

DI Atkins and DS Evans were sat together, talking through everything they knew, all the information they had gathered, the people they had interviewed and tried beyond hope to solve the puzzle, put pieces together, to connect the evening and what had exactly happened. They tried to order events by timings, put people where they said they had been, to almost exactly live the evening that Macy had lived.

Just as they were doing that, the door knocked and the guy that had been trawling through the CCTV entered.

"Hello, Pete," said DI Atkins looking up from her mountain of files. "What you got for us?"

"Hi, Leanne," Pete then nodded at DS Evans "if I'm honest, not too much, but there is this." He moved closer and put the disc into the computer.

DI Atkins and DS Evans watched closely as they surveyed the evening outside the pub. People entered, people left, people stood outside smoking. They saw Macy arrive and wait on the bench waiting for her friends.

They saw Guy and his work colleagues begin there evening and they saw Billy Tomlin and his crew turn up for their rowdy, drink fuelled night. All was as they had thought, nothing out of the ordinary.

Pete then took the disc out and inserted another one. This one showed the bus stop and bus route. They observed Macy getting on the bus and the others all push in front of Mr Denver.

"Now, look carefully," Pete and the officers moved in closer to the screen. It was fuzzy but they could make out the picture.

"This is the bus stop where Macy got off." They watched as she came into view along the road. They also saw Billy Tomlin swaying across the road.

DI Atkins and DS Evans looked blank but focused intently on what Pete was saying, "See here, can you make out a large vehicle, it seems to be speeding, then brakes as Billy crosses the road." The officers looked at one another, this proves Billy was telling the truth.

"Now look, instead of speeding up again, it is crawling along really slowly and whoever it is only has his half beam headlights on now. Macy would have been walking along the pavement. The vehicle now comes out of view as if it has turned left. Turned left towards Macy's block of flats."

DI Atkins felt like she couldn't breathe, Pete could be onto something here. Her adrenalin was pounding.

Pete carried on, swapping discs over again, "So, I went into the Admiral Arms and asked if they used CCTV in their car park. The landlord said they did but it was an ancient system but we were welcome to look at it."

The screen was blurry and you could just make out the car park. Pete put his finger on the screen. "See here, you can just make out a large vehicle, parked here in the car park. I think a van of some sort, but it is the same size and shape of the vehicle crawling along near Macy's route home."

There was silence as all three of them studied the picture that Pete had paused.

"I reckon," he said, "that whoever attacked Macy was in the pub that night and for whatever reason, watched and followed her home and carried out this evil act. I think all you need to do now is find out who that van belongs to and you have your man."

DI Atkins flung down her pen so hard that it bounced across the desk and onto the floor. "Bingo!" she said "I could kiss you Pete, that is excellent work, well done."

"Nah you don't have to kiss me, guv, I'm a married man!"

All three of them chuckled then, glad to have a breakthrough and a bit of light relief.

Chapter 29

Macy's hand shook as she picked up the newspaper in the newsagents nearby her office. She couldn't look at the headline yet, she felt all hot and clammy and wondered if she looked like a woman that had been raped. Would the guy behind the counter put two and two together and know that she was the girl this had happened to?

No, don't be stupid, she told herself, you're just buying the local paper, just like any old Joe Bloggs, just like numerous people would today.

Macy handed over the money, said a quick thank you and almost ran out of the door. Still unable to look at the paper, she shoved it under her arm and walked through the main door and to her office.

Glad that no one was around, she somehow found the courage to read the story about her. DI Atkins could be trusted, her name was not mentioned once. Macy felt so relieved about this but it almost felt surreal that what she was reading was about her. She scanned each word, each sentence, each paragraph over and over again. Her hands clenched around the paper and big tears fell down her cheeks.

She didn't know just how long she had sat there like that, but she did know she only began to feel better when she felt Harry's arm around her.

Harry gestured her into the privacy of his own office and let her sit for a bit, not saying a word just putting his protective arm around her. Macy let it all out then: big sobs followed by big tears running down her face, followed by a wet tissue mopping them up.

Harry had gathered up the newspaper too. "You don't need to look at that again," he said, "you've read it now and it's done."

He moved away from Macy and placed the paper in the drawer in his desk. "There, gone, disappeared." Macy managed a small smile amid the tears.

"I've got some filing here that needs doing, it needs sorting and placing in that filing cabinet," he pointed to the big grey cabinet in the corner of his office. "It may take some time but I figure that you would sooner be in here, than out there today." He looked at the desks outside of his office that were beginning to fill up with all his employees.

Macy wiped her eyes and stood up. Harry was right (again), she would prefer the safety of his office this morning. "Right, best get to it then," she said assertively. Harry grinned, he would look at that paper later, he thought.

Katie pulled up outside the police station. She had no idea if she was doing the right thing but the article in the paper had played on her mind all day. She didn't want to waste the police officers' time but if she didn't say what had happened to her, it would be on her conscience forever if in some way it was connected with this crime and she hadn't done anything.

Walking up to the front desk, she felt her mouth go dry and her legs shake slightly. She was out of her comfort zone here.

"Er, hello," Katie mumbled, feeling it hard to get the words to come out of her mouth.

The guy looked up, expecting her to continue but she hesitated. Looking around one more time, Katie knew she had to do this. "Er, I've come to speak to someone about this," she pulled the newspaper out of her bag and pointed to the article, "I may have some information regarding this crime."

Katie was told to take a seat and it wasn't long before a smart lady who introduced herself as DI Atkins came and took her into one of the interview rooms, she guessed. The women were soon joined by another officer, DS Evans.

Katie put the newspaper on the table. "It's about this," she said, placing her hand over the article.

"Go on," replied DI Atkins.

"Well, I don't know if its connected or not but something similar happened to me a few days ago. Nothing on the scale of this poor girl but I felt I had to come and tell you, just in case it's the same guy."

"Whether its connected or not, you have done the right thing by coming here," reassured DS Evans to Katie. She went on to tell of her ordeal, being followed, the guy coming up behind her and when she told the officers that he had called out the name Macy, she felt the atmosphere change in an instant.

Both officers had sat upright in their chairs and she had noticed a knowing glance between the two of them. "He kept on repeating the name as if he thought I was this woman," continued Katie.

She informed them that he had made her feel scared and vulnerable and that she had felt the need to run all the way home.

DI Atkins lifted her pen from her notepad. "You said this man was driving a van before he got out and came up to you."

"Yes, he was," answered Katie.

"Can you remember what colour the van was?"

"Definitely, it was blue, I'm 100% sure on that."

DI Atkins and DS Evans glanced again at one another. Cleaning up a few other matters, DI Atkins looked at Katie and said, "You have been most helpful, we are extremely grateful that you have brought this incident to our attention. You handled the situation superbly, how are you now?"

"Well I have to admit, I do look over my shoulder when I'm walking on my own now, but I'll be OK. I was initially very frightened and shook up but those feelings are waring away now gradually."

"Look, here is my number, if you need to talk, feel you are in any kind of danger or have any more information on this incident, please do not hesitate to call me and just to re-assure you, we will deal with this."

DI Atkins handed Katie her card with the relevant numbers on.

"Thank you," replied Katie, "and I am glad I came now, I feel a big weight has lifted from me, now that I have told somebody."

She got up and left the room, feeling much lighter than when she entered.

"Well, well, well," said DI Atkins, twisting on her chair to face DS Evans, "the man with the van pops up again and he clearly knows Macy."

Chapter 30

Lou waited outside the interview room. Three other people, two men and one woman sat beside her and opposite her.

She fiddled with her handbag strap which was perched on her lap, her hands were clammy as she desperately tried to retain every piece of information she felt she needed to know to get her through the interview.

She had chosen to wear a smart black pair of trousers and a pink blouse with small white flowers on it.

Lou had revised all she could and now this was it. It hadn't always been easy to concentrate, with what had happened to Macy. She played on Lou's mind constantly and she needed to be there for her friend.

Bringing her out of her thoughts, came a deep voice, "Louisa Carter?"

Lou struggled to get her bag over her shoulder as she got up and replied, "Yes, that's me."

"Follow me," said the well-groomed, suited man, Chairman of the Health Trust whom Lou worked for.

He showed her into a room where three others sat behind a big desk, to which, papers, jugs of water and glasses aligned.

Lou took a seat in front of the interviewers as the man who had seen her in also sat down.

One by one they introduced themselves and Lou tried to remember to smile, show an air of confidence and hoped that she would be able to answer the questions that they were about to fire at her.

Billy had just finished work and had collected the newspaper on his way home. Something to read whilst having his dinner tonight. Walking along, he flicked it over to read the sport, but before he did, something caught his eye on the front of the paper:

LOCAL GIRL IN RAPE SHOCK.

Billy read on, now literally standing still on the pavement. This was what he had been questioned about, Christ this was serious.

People weaved in and around him on the street and he was aware that other pedestrians were cursing him for standing dead still, in their way, he heard people tut and mutter but for some reason he couldn't move. He felt dirty, not that he had done anything wrong but ashamed that he had been associated in some way with the girl, involved in something so evil, so awful. He hoped more than anything that the officers caught the bastard that had done this.

Lou closed the door to the interview room behind her and finally breathed out. She had done her best, she had answered all their questions, put forward ideas and tried to sell herself as the best candidate for the job.

She would find out in the next week, she had been told, whether she had been successful or not.

She headed to the car park and to her car. Switching on her phone, which of course she had turned off during her interview, it beeped as she eased herself into her car.

Reaching over to put her bag on the back seat, she glanced at her phone to see it was a text from Ritchie. Opening up the message, it read:

HI LOU, HOW'S THINGS? HOPE INTERVIEW GOES WELL. MISSING YOU AND MACY, IF BOTH UP TO IT, COME TO MINE FOR DRINKS ON FRIDAY? (OBS PUB OUT OF THE QUESTION) I'LL LEAVE IT TO YOU TO ASK MACY, AS I DON'T WANT TO KEEP BOTHERING HER. XX

Lou gathered her thoughts, poor Ritchie, he had kinda been out of the loop since this had happened. Macy obviously confiding in her much more, which was understandable she guessed.

He was right though, going to the Admiral Arms was definitely out of the question at the moment. She would speak to Macy when she got home but it would be nice for all of them to get together again like they had used to.

She started the car and headed home.

Chapter 31

Harry had waited until everyone had left the office, to take the newspaper out of his drawer. It had been in there since this morning and only now had felt the right opportunity for him to read it.

He felt a lump in his throat, as he read through the article. Sure, he had read things like this many a time, seen crime documentaries on TV about evil human beings, subjecting women to all sorts but never had he seen it in black and white about someone he knew, someone he was close to and saw most days of his life.

Harry had been amazed by Macy. She was a strong woman. This would have destroyed most, but she had dealt with it, returned to work and had done her upmost to carry on and not let whoever had done this to her, win.

He had admired her strength and resilience and prayed that the police involved would solve this and allow Macy closure to this awful period in her life.

Using his hands, he screwed the paper up into a ball, venting all of his anger into squashing it up smaller and tighter. He didn't want Beryl to read it, too upsetting for her. Harry threw it then – a big, strong, decisive throw across his desk and into the waste paper bin.

That's where the scumbag who did this to Macy belonged. At the bottom of the rubbish bin, the lowest of the low.

DI Atkins and DS Evans had worked tirelessly, going back over every detail of the case. They were so nearly there. Evidence was mounting up, suspects ruled out, they had gone through the night again, piecing together the minutes, the seconds even. Dissecting Macy's life, her friends, her job and her wellbeing.

DI Atkins knew only too well that it is a commonly known fact that in most cases the victims know their attackers and all their suspects had been strangers to Macy and had had 100% alibis. So now they were focusing on all those that knew Macy.

DI Atkins sighed, at least it was Friday tomorrow, although an officer's work never stopped at the weekends. Time to go home now and see what tomorrow would bring.

Lou got off the phone to Macy, she had been upset over the newspaper incident and Lou had tried to calm her down. To reassure her no one outside her immediate social circle knew it was her, that she was the victim.

Lou had tried to take her mind off the matter by telling her about her interview and about Ritchie's text.

Macy had thought it was a good idea, she had missed the three of them getting together and it would be a good chance to take her mind off everything.

Lou had offered to pick her up. She would leave her car at Ritchie's so she could have a couple of drinks and they would get a cab home. That way she could see Macy get dropped off right by the entrance to her flat.

Lou texted Ritchie to say they would be there. She was looking forward to a good old catch up with her friends, especially after the stress of her interview and she was sure it would do Macy good too.

Lou hadn't seen the newspaper article; she didn't want to either. She wasn't sure if she could handle seeing it in black and white. Those journalists always exaggerated and made things up, no, she would stick with what Macy had told her, the facts, and not look at the article.

Katie locked her front door behind her, bolted it and double locked it with the key. Ever since she had been to the police Station, she had been a bag of nerves.

Looking over her shoulder in the street, almost running home each day and even looking down the corridors at work to see if anyone was lurking about.

She was pleased she had gone to the police with her information but it was just the way the officers had looked at one another when she had said about the van. She just knew it was all connected with that rape case and it frightened her. She knew they were still looking for the man. The thought that she could have been raped and attacked, she just couldn't bear thinking about.

Katie hoped that the police would catch him soon and she could rest easy again.

Ritchie heard his phone ping in his bedroom. Picking it up, he saw it was a text from Lou. Opening up the message, he read that the girls were up for tomorrow night. He grinned; he was pleased. It would be nice to see them both, especially Macy. His mood lifted at that thought.

Chapter 32

Macy got up, glad it was Friday, she felt brighter than yesterday and she was looking forward to seeing Lou and Ritchie tonight.

She felt bad for Ritchie; it had somehow felt awkward to confide in him over the past weeks, preferring to tell Lou everything instead. She was sure she could have gone to him; he had texted her often enough to see how she was. She probably could have cried on his shoulder and he would have been there for her, but she had felt almost embarrassed to pour out her feelings to him.

As Macy looked at herself in the mirror, she hoped this hadn't put a strain on their friendship. She would chat with him tonight, make it all OK again.

Pulling a bright crimson top over her head, she felt like her old self again. Alive and in control and ready to enjoy tonight like they used to.

DI Atkins had allowed herself a 30 minutes lie-in this morning, and now in the office, she allowed herself time to drink her coffee. She looked at the whiteboard with all its photos, timelines, different coloured writing on it, all of it connected in some way. All of it about one evening. She just had to find that vital clue that pieced it together completely and she would, she was certain of that.

Macy placed her knife and fork onto her plate. Wow, that burger was delicious and it would help soak up some of the alcohol she would be drinking tonight.

Harry had treated her to lunch today; it was the first time she had been in a pub since the attack, so she had been dubious at first, but after some gentle persuasion from Harry and the thought of a nice hearty meal, she had gone and it hadn't been as bad as she had thought.

Herself and Harry had chatted about nothing in particular and she had relaxed. She hadn't been tense, she hadn't watched every person who came through the door or watched who was at the bar. She had been herself and found that she was smiling, laughing instead of being sombre or crying. Macy had needed this and she had needed the protection of Harry to help her.

"Right, come on Macy, we can't stay here all afternoon, we have work to do," said Harry, pulling on his suit jacket.

"Coming," replied Macy. She would sort through her paperwork and emails and then head home to get ready for tonight. She knew she wasn't going 'out' out, but she still wanted to look her best, casual but smart and that needed careful planning, she grinned to herself.

DI Atkins ran into the main office.

"Everyone," she shouted. The room went silent, all eyes were on the woman by the whiteboard.

Whilst being in her office, DI Atkins had replayed all the interviews with everyone in her head and it was then that it had come to her.

She had thought back to when she had seen Ritchie at his flat. Whilst walking back to her car, she passed the car park to his flats and had noticed a blue van, the same blue van that was in the car park of the pub and in the CCTV footage and most probably the one that that had kerb crawled Katie Smith. She had checked number plates, checked the CCTV again and replayed that afternoon in her mind. He had slightly unnerved her when she had seen him watching her from his window, she wouldn't lie.

Telling her colleagues all of this, she rubbed out everything on the board apart from his name. punching her pen hard on his name, she said, "This is the man that attacked and raped his so-called friend on that Friday night and this is the man that frightened Katie Smith. I need back up at his home ASAP. Myself and DS Evans are wrapping this case up and arresting him now. Well done everyone for your hard work, patience and dedication. Let's *go* get him!"

Chapter 33

Macy had decided on dark blue jeans and a pink, long sleeved top with some lace on for tonight. She looked in the mirror, smart but casual. She was just tying her hair back into a ponytail when she heard the beep of Lou's car horn.

Grabbing her handbag and a bottle of wine, she was feeling ready for a fun and chilled night with her two best friends.

They arrived at Ritchie's fairly quickly and Macy hadn't needed to feel uncomfortable at all. He was fine, said he understood why she had been distant and that all he wanted was for her to be OK.

The three of them laughed, drank and joked and Macy could feel herself loosening up and relaxing. She had missed this. There was nothing better than being with friends.

As Ritchie topped up her glass with wine, she vowed she would not waste anymore of her time, tears and sadness on the scumbag that had attacked her. She didn't owe him any of those feelings and she wasn't going to allow him to take anymore of her life.

She took a big sip of wine, to new beginnings and recapturing the old Macy too.

The girls listened to Ritchie's latest catastrophes at work and laughed and giggled, then they listened to Lou's funny patient stories and Macy told them about Harry and her work.

This was what it was all about, catching up with each other and sharing stories, sharing lives.

The officers sprang into action, one big police van sat outside the entrance to Ritchie's flat and DI Atkins had two police officers standing round the back at a fire exit, just in case he decided to make a run for it.

DI Atkins and DS Evans parked up, too, in front of the entrance. "Ready?" she asked.

"Definitely," he replied.

Macy looked at her watch, goodness they had only been here a short while but the wine was flowing. Ritchie had had his quota and was now drinking lemonade.

"Just going to the ladies," revealed Macy, getting up from the comfy arm chair and heading to the bathroom.

She closed and locked the door behind her.

Washing her hands, she looked into the mirror above the sink, her ponytail needed re-doing. As she pulled out the scrunch, her arm brushed her ear, causing one of her earrings to fall out. Shit! Where had it rolled too? She couldn't see it anywhere.

Letting her hair fall loose, she scoured the bathroom floor. No sign of the small gold hoop anywhere. She looked under the bathmat, still no sign of it.

Macy twisted round in a circle, her eyes on the floor, looking for anything that glistened – nothing.

She went back to the sink and tied her hair back now. Wait a minute – could it have rolled under the cupboard below the sink? She bent down to have a look.

Obstructing her view, to see right the way down, was something black, hanging out of the cupboard. Macy tried to move it, but it was wedged. She hated going through people's belongings but she needed to open the door of the cupboard to push whatever it was back in, to be able to see under it. She was sure Ritchie wouldn't mind. She opened the door and it fell out. Damn!

Macy bent to pick it up, and had to put her hand to her mouth to stifle her scream!

She instantly felt cold and sick to the stomach. No way! Please God, no way!

On the floor lay a black leather glove. Macy had a flash-back to when she was attacked. The man had grabbed her round the mouth with a black glove. She could still sense the smell of it. In fact, that was the last thing she had remembered before waking up on the grass.

Her hand shook as she reached for the glove and she could see the other glove now in the cupboard. Her eyes filling up with tears now, she closed them, huge teardrops running down her face.

Macy slowly brought the glove to her face and sniffed. She heaved and throwing the glove down, rushed to the toilet and threw up.

It was the same smell, a smell she would never forget. No, this could not be happening. Not Ritchie, he was meant to be her friend. He had acted completely normal, how could he if he was her attacker?

She put the gloves back, her lost earring all forgotten now and washed her face.

What the hell was she going to do? She needed to get out, but if he knew that she knew, she could make things worse.

Or was this his plan? Get her into his flat and rape her again or worse still, was he going to attack Lou as well?

"You OK in there?" Lou shouted.

Aware she must have been in there some time now, Macy answered, "Yeah Lou, just re-doing my hair."

She had to act normal, carry on with the evening, then get herself and Lou out and get to DI Atkins. How could she act normal though? She wanted to kill him! She felt as if she might faint, her legs like jelly and her stomach tied in knots. Her breathing was fast and intense.

Come on, Macy, you can get through this, she thought, as she left the bathroom and entered back into the lounge.

Lou and Ritchie were chatting about some box set they were both watching. Macy studied them both. Surely Lou wasn't in on this? Her best friend, had she been set up?

No, that was absurd. Macy had watched Lou support her, had seen her cry with her and had gone with her to the police, been there while she had been examined. Lou had been genuinely shocked and upset by all of this. Macy pushed that thought to the back of her head.

She took a sip of wine and observed Ritchie. Looking at him now, she had to check in her head what had really just happened in the bathroom.

Was she going mad? Had the drink got to her? No, she had smelt the glove. This was real.

He didn't look like a rapist, far from it, he had a really angelic-looking face. He was laughing and it took Macy everything she had, not to go over to him and spit in his face. She wanted to shout and scream, but she knew she had to sit tight and bide her time. She realised, looking down that her free hand was clenched and fist-like.

Macy didn't have to bide her time for long, the three of them jumped out of their skin as Ritchie's front door was battered open and in walked DI Atkins and DS Evans accompanied by two policemen.

Stunned that the two girls were there, DI Atkins arrested Ritchie and one of the policemen handcuffed him. He was screaming, "No, no, I did not do this." He was pleading even, not to be taken away, over and over again shouting, "No!"

Poor Lou looked as if she had seen a ghost and all the while Macy sat glued to the spot. Numb, unable to move, the last words she heard Ritchie say was, "I did not do this to you, Macy" and then silence, as he was taken by DS Evans out onto the landing and down the stairs.

One policeman stayed in the flat with DI Atkins. "I'm sorry, Macy and Lou, that you had to witness that. CCTV picked up his van and another girl came forward with important information that linked the two cases."

"What, so he raped someone else too?" asked Lou, her voice quiet and shaky.

"Not quite, but he frightened a girl and for some reason thought she was Macy," replied DI Atkins.

"This doesn't make any sense," Lou held her head in her hands.

The policeman was going through all of Ritchie's possessions.

"Gloves," said Macy, coming out of her daze.

"Pardon?" DI Atkins turned to her.

"Gloves, in the bathroom cupboard, you're looking for evidence and there you will find it but I've touched them and my fingerprints will be on them. In some cruel twist of fate, I found them and figured out Ritchie was my attacker just before you turned up."

DI Atkins looked at Macy, now being consoled by Lou. Two friends betrayed and let down by someone they had trusted. Her heart went out to them, especially Macy.

She moved into the kitchen, on the shelf was a mixture of tablets and pills. Wearing plastic gloves, she removed them and beckoned Lou into the kitchen. "Why was he taking so many pills?"

Lou explained about the accident and the way they had become friends with her nursing him back to health.

Lou looked at the jars of tablets, studying them carefully. She began to realise something. Some of these tablets were not compatible with each other. If Ritchie was taking these all together, he would most definitely be suffering from severe blackouts from time to time. The strength of the dosage and the amount of tablets would be extremely dangerous to a human being. Who had prescribed these to Ritchie and was he having a blackout when he attacked Macy?

This was more complex than they at first thought. DI Atkins realized, back at the station.

The gloves were being examined as were all the tablets, Ritchie Bart was in a cell and really, there was not much they could do until the morning. DI Atkins tidied up her desk and headed for home, having sent DS Evans home earlier.

Macy was at Lou's, sleeping on the sofa, well sleeping was an understatement. She wouldn't get any of that tonight. This whole situation seemed so surreal.

Macy just couldn't work it all out. She had trusted Ritchie; how could he do this to her? Lou had explained about the blackouts, could it be true, that he wouldn't even remember raping her? She didn't know what was worse.

Lou had offered to sit with her all night but Macy had insisted that she go to bed. She needed time alone with her thoughts, her fears and her tears. Still in her clothes from the evening with a blanket around her, Macy tried to make sense of it all. Who was this other girl and why did he think she was her? Was that another 'blackout' moment?

She had so many questions and so little answers. In her mind, she had thought that when her attacker had been found and arrested, she would feel better, more at ease, but this, this had just made it ten times worse. Ritchie, Ritchie, her friend, a person she had confided in only tonight. Feeling as if her mind was spinning out of control, Macy finally gave in and drifted off to sleep.

Ritchie sat on the hard, uncomfortable bed in the tiny, square cell. He had jumped when the door had shut behind him. The noise of it being loud, echoey and so final.

His head in his hands, he wondered how on earth had he gotten here. He couldn't have attacked Macy; she was his friend, but he did know that he did have times when he felt out of it, like his head was on somebody else's body and he didn't know why.

Ritchie looked around at the plain white walls, the big metal door and the dirty, grubby toilet. What had started out as a perfectly normal and pleasant evening, had now turned into one big horrible nightmare.

He laid down now, on the hard mattress. They were going to question him tomorrow, so he had better try and get some sleep. He shut his eyes tight, but he knew there was no way he was going to sleep tonight.

Chapter 34

DI Atkins was in the office early the next morning. She was in the forensics lab with DS Evans who had also come in early today.

"Results from the gloves," explained Judy, the forensic scientist officer. "The DNA proves it is a match with Ritchie and Macy and on closer inspection of inside the glove, we found a single strand of long brown hair." Both officers were not in any doubt that it was Macy's hair.

Picking up the bag of medicines, Judy said, "These, you will need to get a doctor's advice on, but I can confirm that each of the jars have Ritchie's finger prints on."

"Thanks, Judy, for your help." DI Atkins took the bags of evidence and headed back to her office followed by DS Evans. "Let's go see the police doctor," she said, "let Ritchie sweat a bit before we question him and anyhow we need to get the low down on all his meds."

"OK, guv, this should be interesting," he replied.

Down where the cells were, it was bleak and cold and DI Atkins knew for certain that she wouldn't like to be held up in one all night. They found the doctor in his room, getting ready to go home after being on the night shift.

"Sorry doc, we've got a job for you before you go home," said DI Atkins plonking the bag of pills down on his desk.

The doctor sighed, "I must say you have impeccable timing!" He picked up the bag, observing the contents inside. "These were all being taken by one person?" he asked.

"Yes," replied DI Atkins, "we are interested to know the side effects, dosage, brain activity, anything you can tell us about these drugs."

"Guess my bacon sandwich and sleep will have to wait then, give me an hour and I'll find out everything I can."

"You're a star and I'll pay for your bacon sarnie!" she winked.

Macy woke with a start, sweating and feeling clammy. Did last night really happen or had she dreamt it? It only took her a few seconds to realise that none of this was a dream. Her stomach was in knots and her eyes were sore from the lack of sleep and crying.

Slowly she got up and could hear Lou was up too. "Morning," the girls said in unison and both of them burst into tears, flinging their arms around one another, both still in total disbelief at what had happened last night.

Lou hadn't slept much either and luckily she wasn't in work today. She was struggling to believe that Ritchie could have done this to Macy, but the evidence was there with the gloves and obviously the police knew what they were doing, but he had genuinely looked shocked and heartbroken when they charged him and took him away or, Lou thought, was he just heartbroken that he had been found out! Had he attacked other women and had she been next on his list?

Wiping their tears away, Lou said, "I'll put the kettle on, think we need a tea." The girls sat, talking for ages in their pyjamas, holding onto the comfort of the hot mug of tea, trying to make sense of it all.

The hour passed quickly and the officers made their way back down to the cells to see what the doctor had found out about all the drugs Ritchie had been taking. DI Atkins knocked on the door, waited for the nod to enter and walked through the door. DS Evans followed.

They sat opposite the doctor, all of Ritchie Bart's medicines were on the desk. "What you got for us then?"

"Well, it's quite simple really, looking at all these drugs and the dosages, all these tablets taken together would yes, take away all of Mr Bart's pain but it would also cause blackouts, bouts of paranoia and sometimes schizophrenic traits. I'm guessing whoever prescribed these," he held up one jar of pills, "did not realise Mr Bart was taking all these other tablets. Sometimes, consultants, doctors and the hospital don't read all the patients notes properly or Mr Bart has lied about what medication he is on and combined, has taken lethal dosages of all tablets together."

The doctor continued, "I would conclude looking at this case, that the events that happened were when Mr Bart was under the influence of these tablets and he was probably unaware of his actions. I am confident enough to stand up in court and testify."

The officers looked at one another. They still had Ritchie to interview and to hear and watch his side of the story but the doctor had been pretty adamant.

"Thank you so much, Doc, you have been really helpful." DI Atkins reached into her back pocket and pulled out a five-pound note. Placing it on the doctor's desk, "For your bacon sandwich," she smirked!

Chapter 35

Ritchie was led into the interview room by a tall, broad policeman and told to sit. His palms were sweaty and he felt empty and numb. His body ached, which he wasn't sure was down to the fact of only being given paracetamol and not his usual tablets or down to the fact that he was scared stiff.

He had no idea what was about to happen or what the officers were going to ask him. He just had to tell the truth. His mouth was so dry, he wondered if he would be able to get his words out even.

DI Atkins and DS Evans entered the room. They sat opposite Ritchie and the female officer looked ready for action, he thought. Ritchie trembled, apart from his accident, this was fast becoming the worse time of his life.

"Simple question to start with, Mr Bart," said DI Atkins. "Did you attack and rape Macy Reynolds, then leave her hurt and unconscious on the grass by her flat?"

"No, I didn't." Ritchie stammered and was so hoarse that the words struggled to come out. He had to clench his hands together on his lap for fear of them shaking vigorously.

"On the evidence that we have, that does not seem to be the correct answer, Mr Bart." He stared at the officers in front of him. Evidence, what evidence? He had gone out for a drink that night with his friends, dropped Lou home and then gone home himself, hadn't he?

DS Evans pulled open a folder and positioned photographic pictures of Ritchie's van, firstly in the street near Macy's then parked up even nearer to Macy's flat.

"Is this not you driving your van on the evening of Macy's attack and is this not your van parked up by Macy's home?"

Ritchie looked intently at the photos and was told to look at the date and time of each photo carefully too. He couldn't deny any of it but he didn't remember it either.

"Let's talk about your relationship with Macy," continued DI Atkins. "You're friends with her?"

Ritchie nodded. "Would you like to be more than just friends with her? Did she give you the brush off? More than once? Did you get angry and think, I'm going to have her anyway? Is that why you raped her, when you had had enough of her pushing you away?"

DI Atkins voice was getting louder and Ritchie was beginning to get flustered.

"Yes, no, no, I like her and admit I fancy her but no, no no!" Ritchie banged the desk with his fist and then put his head in his arms.

Gathering his thoughts, he looked up, and speaking slightly more calmly now, he said, "Yes, I found her attractive and sometimes I did wonder if there could be a relationship there but I have never come on to her." He was pleading now but the photos on the desk told another story and he didn't know how.

DI Atkins was ready for another go. "Katie Smith, do you know her?"

"Who?" he replied, puzzled.

"She made a complaint about you, that you were kerb crawling, shouting out Macy's name. You grabbed her and intimidated her."

Ritchie couldn't believe what he was hearing, he didn't know anyone called Katie Smith, let alone grab her in the street.

"Maybe this will jog your memory," said DI Atkins as she slammed down a photo of Katie on the desk.

Ritchie looked long and hard at it. He was certain he did not know her. Granted, she had long hair like Macy and a similar-shape face but he was sure he wouldn't get the two people confused, would he?

"I don't know her and I really don't know what's going on here. I think I might be being set up."

He was clutching at straws now, he felt so confused. Why was his van near Macy's flat and who the hell was this girl who was claiming he had attacked her as well?

Ritchie's head was spinning and he took a mouthful of water from the plastic cup that had been on the desk when he had entered earlier. That felt like ages ago; he didn't know what to say or do. He was a crumbling mess.

"So, Mr Bart, just to clarify, you are telling us that you did not rape Macy Reynolds or intimidate Katie Smith even when we have substantial evidence sitting right here on this desk?"

Ritchie looked DI Atkins straight in the eyes. He noticed that they were begging for his voice to be heard.

"I did not do anything to either of those women."

"OK we will end it there," she said gathering up the stuff and nodding to the officer by the door to take Ritchie back to his cell.

Once gone, DI Atkins turned to DS Evans. "We'll tackle the question of the pills and gloves tomorrow, but my guess is the Doc is right, Mr Bart has been having blackouts and his subconscious is playing tricks on him. I actually believe, that he believes he did not do this to either of the women. This is going to be a difficult one."

"Agreed," replied DS Evans, deep in thought.

Chapter 36

Macy and Lou spent the day chatting and sobbing with each other. They both questioned how this could have happened and questioned their own stupidity of how they could have been so close to Ritchie and not known he was capable of rape. You just didn't know anyone these days.

Lou thought about all the time she had cared for Ritchie after his accident. She had shown him friendship, love, compassion and above all professionalism and then allowed him to become one of her closest friends along with Macy. Would Macy blame her? After all, she was the one that had welcomed him into her life and introduced him to Macy. Her stomach trembled.

A voice inside her niggled away and she couldn't get out of her head the amount of tablets he was taking. All of them together would not have been a good idea. Had he been under the influence of all these drugs when he attacked Macy? Was he unaware of what he had done? She needed answers and really hoped she and especially Macy would get them.

Macy felt numb; when you thought you could trust someone and they betray you like this. She let her mind wander back to the day she had met Ritchie. Lou had invited her to join them for coffee in a local coffee shop.

When she had first set eyes on him, she had seen a man on crutches, thin and drawn, having not long had his accident and been let out of hospital to recover.

Ritchie had been friendly and polite and she had felt a connection straight away. He had been easy to chat to and he had a good sense of humour. She remembered how they had all laughed in that coffee shop that day and had been in there way longer than they had all anticipated.

How had it gone from that to this, Macy wondered, shuddering at the thought of finding those gloves. She knew there was some indication that he hadn't known what he was doing because of the amount of medication he was taking, but none the less, her so-called friend had betrayed her beyond belief and she could never face him or forgive him for the foreseeable future.

It had been a long and tiring day for DI Atkins, and she was glad to get home. Flinging her shoes off and putting her briefcase down in the hallway, she entered the kitchen and placed the Chinese takeaway bag on the work surface. She hadn't fancied cooking tonight so she had picked up a Chow Mein on the way home.

Collecting a plate and wine glass from the draining board by the sink, DI Atkins poured herself a large glass of red wine and dished up her noodles.

Finally, she sat down on the chair and placed her plate on the table but kept hold of the glass and took a big swig of wine. Boy! She needed that!

She had come down hard on Mr Bart today and he had been crushed by the pressure of it all. In a strange way she did feel sorry for him. but the evidence, DNA, photos and Katie

Smith were 100% proof that he had committed these crimes, though she herself, was 99% sure he was unaware of this.

He had never been in trouble with the law before and had not seemed to be covering anything up. He had almost been pleading with her towards the end of the interview.

It was all such a sad state of affairs, a man who, high on medication, had ruined a life of a friend, had scared the life out of a stranger in the street and had destroyed another friendship in Lou and it was looking very likely that he had destroyed his own life too.

Although he would plead his innocence, they would have to charge him.

She thought back to Howard Denver and saw that Ritchie Bart would almost have to live his life like him. Being pointed at in the street, sneered at, labelled. She didn't think that Ritchie was a bad man, Macy had never once pointed the finger at him.

How must she feel, she had been betrayed by someone she thought she could rely on.

Taking another gulp of wine, it was going to be a long night.

Chapter 37

Ritchie had had a rough night; the cell was cold, other inmates were loud, the bed was uncomfortable and the food inedible. What did he expect though, this wasn't a hotel.

He put his uneaten breakfast tray on the floor and wondered what the hell today would bring.

DI Atkins had briefed her team earlier this morning and was getting ready to speak with Mr Bart again. DS Evans was in the office holding the forensic bag containing the gloves.

"Ready for round two?" he said.

"Yeah, this is complex though, so not straight forward. I have a feeling we are going to charge a man with rape who has absolutely no recollection of doing it."

They sighed and made their way to the interview room. Ritchie was already in there when the officers arrived.

DI Atkins observed that he looked scared stiff and that his whole body looked tense. She would go easier on him today.

She started off with general chit chat, just to put him at ease. Then said, "Mr Bart, as you are still claiming that you are innocent from these crimes, we have two other matters to talk to you about. Firstly, these gloves…"

DS Evans took the gloves from the bag and placed them on the desk. Ritchie stared at them.

"Do you recognise these?"

"Yes," he said, his voice shaking slightly, "I used to wear them when I drove my motorbike, before my accident."

"These gloves, Mr Bart, were used to grab Macy Reynolds around the face, push her to the ground and rape her."

Ritchie was white with fear.

"Then Macy Reynolds found these gloves in your flat stuffed under the sink cupboard in your bathroom. Can you tell me how they got there please?"

"I don't know," stuttered Ritchie, "I found them in my van and remember taking them into the flat but I don't know how she found them in the bathroom. I didn't put them there, I'm sure."

"He didn't say it but he wondered if they had been planted there, but why?"

"Are you sure, Mr Bart?" questioned DI Atkins.

"I'm telling the truth, officer."

She put the gloves back into the bag and took out a sheet with all the medication printed on it. *Now for the complicated bit. Here goes*, she thought.

"Mr Bart, here is a list of all the medication you take," she turned the paper around so he could see it. "Is this correct?"

Ritchie studied it. "Yes, that's all my drugs. They're all kept in the kitchen in my flat. I have to take them, coz after my accident, the pain and the flashbacks. It never went away, so I take these tablets so I can get through each day and hold down a job. I don't drink alcohol now because of this. So, I wasn't drunk on that Friday evening. The landlord will vouch for that."

Ritchie was clinging on to anything that could prove his innocence.

"Who prescribed all this medication?" piped in DS Evans.

"The hospital and the doctors," replied Ritchie.

"And did either of them know what the other had already prescribed?" continued DI Atkins.

"Yes, I assumed so," answered Ritchie, perplexed, "I've always taken any medical forms I have to each appointment and I've always taken anything they have given me."

"When you take these tablets, how do they make you feel?"

"They take the pain away in my leg and hip and that then allows me to drive. Other pills allow me to get a good night's sleep without having the continuous nightmares about the accident. I do sometimes feel drowsy and forgetful with them and sometimes I fall asleep and have no recollection of doing so or what I was doing beforehand, but not all the time."

This was interesting, so Ritchie Bart had just admitted that he sometimes couldn't remember what he was doing and felt drowsy. This was before they had told him about the outcome of all these tablets being examined.

DI Atkins sighed, poor bloke. This job was so not black and white at times.

"Mr Bart, we took your medication to our specialist doctor who examined what would be happening if a person was to take all these tablets. He looked at the quantity, dosage, studied the tablets individually and these were his findings," she paused to look at Mr Bart. He was staring right into her eyes; they were sad and frightened and she felt some pity towards him.

"The doctor concluded that a person of your gender, age, weight and lifestyle would most certainly suffer from mental blackouts and could subconsciously behave in a manner that you would not remember. That you would most likely, on occasions, feel drowsy and nauseous and he was confident that you would pass out and sleep for a long period of time. He was concerned that a person should never have been allowed to take all this medication at one time."

Again, she paused, DS Evans looked at her. Ritchie looked forlorn and both of them, she felt at that time, felt some compassion for Mr Bart, which hardly ever happened at the point where they were about to charge somebody and wrap up the case.

"Therefore, Mr Bart, I believe that subconsciously you wanted Macy Reynolds as more than just a friend and high on all the medication and unaware of your actions, you attacked and raped her that night and then went home and passed out, only to wake up, not knowing what you had done. I am also confident, that again, high on your medication, when driving, you believed you saw Macy which was in fact Katie Smith. When she didn't answer you, you got cross, stopped your van, went over to her, grabbed her and intimidated her, then again woke up to not knowing anything. With this, Mr Bart, and all of the other evidence, I have no choice but to charge you with the rape and assault of Macy Reynolds."

It was at this point that Ritchie cried like a baby, he cried in disbelief and also with the fact that DI Atkins was absolutely right in everything she had said.

Chapter 38

DI Atkins had made a personal visit to Lou's home to inform both girls that they had charged Mr Bart and were now awaiting a trial date. She explained everything and told the girls that her job was almost complete on this case but that she would attend the trial when it happened.

She said that Lou may get called as a witness and told Macy to keep being strong and that if she ever needed her, she was to ring without hesitation.

Macy, still in shock but relieved that Ritchie had been charged, thanked DI Atkins and told her she would be eternally grateful to her and her team for all their hard work and compassion towards her.

DI Atkins left soon after, never one to outstay her welcome. They had offered her tea but she had declined. She had to remember these girls were not her friends, it was sometimes easy to forget that when you worked so closely with people for many weeks.

She had to go back to the station to finalise the paperwork, then she would head off home early today before another case came in.

DS Evans was removing all the photos and clearing the writing off the board when DI Atkins returned. "Another one bites the dust," he said turning towards her.

"Yeah, this has been an interesting case by no means. Lots of secrets unravelled with people, lives turned upside down, lies exposed and the guilty person let down by the medical profession. Who would have thought it?"

"Yes," replied DS Evans, peeling off the blue tac on the back of Macy's photo. Turning it over and looking at her beautiful face, he said, "How do you think she will be now?"

Leaning over and also looking at her photo, taking in her bright brown eyes and soft smooth skin, DI Atkins answered, "I think she will be OK, given time; she has been betrayed in the most bizarre way but she is a strong woman and with Lou and her boss supporting her, I'm sure she will have some high and low times, but she will come out of it OK."

Filing away the photos and forms, DS Evans shut the cabinet hard making DI Atkins flinch somewhat.

She was on her own then in the office, on her own with her own thoughts on the case. You never really knew what happened to these people after the case had concluded. As a police officer you were just there during the worst of it, in the thick of it almost, but she was certain Macy would be fine, or was it that she just wanted her to be, her own personal feelings wanting Macy to have a fairy tale ending.

Chapter 39

Macy had gone home that night, realising that she needed time on her own to let the news of today sink in and have her own thoughts.

She sat on the sofa and smoothed her hands over the soft fabric. Ritchie had sat there on many occasions when they had all met up, either to spend the evening at Macy's or to collect her and Lou and take them out. Had he been watching her then? She never had any clue that he fancied her. They were only ever just friends, no flirting had ever gone on.

She couldn't even bear to think what would have happened if she had got a lift with him that night. Had he been planning it all along? The other girl too, Macy felt for her. Strangers, but held together by one sad situation in their lives.

She had moved by the window now and gazed to where 'it' had happened, the place where her dignity, her personality and her life had shattered into a thousand pieces.

A tear ran down her cheek, she had to build those pieces together again and move on. She couldn't let Ritchie Bart halt her life for any longer. She hoped she would get answers to her questions during the trial but for now she must try to put everything behind her and instead of being a victim, be a survivor.

She pulled the curtains to shut away the view and walked to the mirror looking at her reflection. Out loud she said, "Come on, Macy Reynolds, you can beat this."

The determination in her voice made her know that she would.

Six months on…

Guy took his children into the garden with a football; he was going to have a kick about with them before lunch. "Dad, Dad come on, try and score!" said his youngest getting ready in the goal.

Guy kicked the football and struck the back of the net. "GOOOAALL!!!" he shouted running around the garden, the kids chasing him and pushing him to the ground and clambering over him.

Out of the corner of his eye, he could see his wife looking at them from the kitchen window.

A pang of guilt came across. How stupid had he been to think life would have been better with Claire. This was what counted; time with the children and a happy wife and marriage, not the thrill and excitement of an affair.

Claire had moved on and had left Marshall's which had made it easier for him to forget and carry on with normal life. His wife had never found out and he had never had the guts to tell her, fearing it would lead to the end of their marriage and anyhow some secrets were best kept as that.

Katie stopped at the door to her office in the school. She had to pinch herself sometimes when she saw her name on the gold plaque fixed to the middle of the door. 'KATIE SMITH DEPUTY HEAD'

She entered her office and sat on the plush black leather chair. She hadn't dared believe that she would get the job of

Deputy when she had applied, but the governors and the Head had believed in her and she was determined she wouldn't let them down.

Goodness, how life had changed for her in the last six months. She had put all the business of Ritchie Bart behind her after she had given evidence at his trial. She had brushed herself down and got on with life. She knew that knowing he was behind bars had made it easier for her, but nevertheless, that was old news now. She was looking to the future and getting this job was just the start for her.

Howard stood at the serving hatch ready to dish out today's hot lunch. He loved Tuesdays and Thursdays. Ever since DI Atkins had told him that he was really proved to be innocent, that Susie had admitted everything had been fabricated, he had felt a new lease of life. He didn't have to hide away anymore. Slowly but surely he had built up his confidence and courage and now he volunteered in a women's refuge two days a week. He really enjoyed it and hoped he was of some help to the people who ran it and to the poor women and children who found themselves there.

Howard had made friends and was amazed at himself at how his personality had changed for the better. He was re discovering who he was and was almost the man he was before all this happened.

The ping of the microwave stopped him from daydreaming and he got on with the business of making sure that all the tenants ate well today.

For what seemed like an eternity, Howard now, at last, felt happy and content with life.

The months after Ritchie had been arrested had gone quickly for Lou; she was enjoying her new job in the hospital and her friendship with Macy was now even stronger.

It had taken her a while to get used to giving out orders to the nurses on her ward but gradually she was becoming more confident and she quite enjoyed being in-charge. Lou looked at her watch, ten more minutes break, then back to it.

Macy and herself made more time to meet up with each other and Lou had seen how Macy had slowly returned to her old self. At the beginning it was hard, they would talk about what had happened, reminisce about Ritchie and questioned how this all could have happened. They had cried together as well, but as the weeks turned into months, Lou had recognised that they hardly mentioned Ritchie now and she had watched Macy grow stronger and was now rebuilding her life.

She grinned, she saw much of that in her profession, seeing patients at their lowest ebb, ill and dependent on the hospital system and then seeing them gradually get better and independent again. It was a nice feeling and very rewarding.

It made Lou feel warm inside, knowing that she was helping people. *Right, back to work,* she thought as she swallowed the last mouthful of tea, that was at the bottom of her mug.

Ritchie flinched as the cell door shut behind him. He still couldn't get used to all the noises in here. He sat down on the hard mattress. So, that was the day's fresh air over with, he just had to sit in his cell now until he was let out for dinner.

Ritchie let out a big sigh, how had his life become like this? He still had no recollection of the attack and deeply regretted that he had caused Macy so much pain. The doctors in the prison had changed all his medication so that he no longer suffered from blackouts, seizures and changes in his person-ality. Though now, being stuck in here, he almost wished he could still pass out on a regular basis.

He had been given five years but could serve less for good behaviour.

Ritchie would never forget standing there at the trial, be-ing found guilty. His legs and hands had shaken when the ver-dict was read out and he had felt as if he had been punched in the face, but worse than all those feelings and the realisation that this was now, how he had become, had been the look on Macy's face. A mixture of relief, pain, and hurt all rolled into one. He would never forget that.

Ritchie shuddered as he remembered that day. That was the trouble in here, you had too much time to think. He had been advised to appeal the verdict on the grounds that he hadn't known what he was doing due to the drugs.

Although he didn't like to admit it, he was pinning his hopes on winning it, so that he could be released earlier.

He hated it in here, but he kept his head down and tried not to entertain anything or anybody that could jeopardise his release.

Neither Macy nor Lou had visited him since he was sent down, which he couldn't blame them for, but he did feel there were still things that had been left unsaid. Things that he needed to say to them both, to explain himself properly and to say sorry personally. He knew 'sorry' wasn't enough but he did hope that one day he would get the chance to apologize to them both.

Macy smiled as she walked through the park, heading to the cafe to meet Scott.

Scott was Harry's nephew and they had been seeing each other now for a few weeks. It had been difficult at first but he was so lovely and having known what she had gone through, was willing to take it slowly.

He made her laugh, get butterflies in her stomach and generally feel happy about her life.

She had met him at Beryl's birthday tea party. They had chatted, exchanged numbers and began meeting up a couple of times a week. Sometimes she had to pinch herself to realise that she had woken up from the recent nightmare and that she was really this happy.

Macy had struggled with the trial, reliving it had been really hard and facing Ritchie had been devastating because once being really good friends she was now opposite him in court.

When the guilty verdict had been called out, Macy had felt numb, she didn't cry, she hadn't felt anger, just complete numbness.

She had heard talk on the grapevine, that he was appealing but she had put that to the back of her mind, knowing that right now he was behind bars and she was safe and Scott made her feel safe too.

She spotted him at the cafe, his back towards her, his short dark hair showing off his neckline and shirt collar.

She shivered with happiness. As if knowing she was there behind him, he turned his head and waved.

Life was good, she thought, right now, and she wasn't in a hurry to change that.